West looked at Annabel for a long moment, then seemed to realize he had an audience, and cleared his throat.

"See you later at my place," he said before disappearing through the door. He was back in a heartbeat. "For the cooking lesson," he added.

Annabel felt her cheeks warm but couldn't help the chuckle. Yet as she thought about being alone with West Montgomery in his house, in his kitchen, standing shoulder to shoulder at the counter, the chuckle was replaced by honest-to-goodness fear.

How did you stop yourself from falling for someone you'd never gotten over to begin with?

* * *

Hurley's Homestyle Kitchen:
There's nothing more delicious
than falling in love…

A COWBOY IN THE KITCHEN

BY
MEG MAXWELL

First Published in Great Britain 2016
By Mills & Boon, an imprint of HarperCollins*Publishers*
1 London Bridge Street, London, SE1 9GF

© 2016 Meg Maxwell

ISBN: 978-0-263-91973-8

23-0316

Our policy is to use papers that are natural, renewable and recyclable products and made from wood grown in sustainable forests.The logging and manufacturing processes conform to the legal environmental regulations of the country of origin.

Printed and bound in Spain
by CPI, Barcelona

Meg Maxwell lives on the coast of Maine with her teen-aged son, their beagle and black-and-white cat. When she's not writing, Meg is either reading, at the movies or thinking up new story ideas on her favorite little beach (even in winter) just minutes from her house. Interesting fact: Meg Maxwell is a pseudonym for author Melissa Senate, whose women's fiction titles have been published in over twenty-five countries.

When I was twenty-one years old, I read my first category romance novel: a funny, heartwarming book by Janet Evanovich with—for reasons I forget—a hero running around in a feathered chicken costume. That book hooked me on the genre, though my favorite heroes became cowboys and cops more than six-foot-tall chickens. Since then, I've read thousands more category romances and dedicate my own to all those authors who inspired me and continue to do so, old and new favorites alike.

Chapter One

Barbecued catfish po'boy with Hurley's Homestyle Kitchen's famed spicy slaw would be tonight's special, Annabel Hurley decided—until all thought poofed from her head with a glance out the window. She ducked behind the industrial-sized silver mixing bowl, a glob of biscuit batter falling from the wooden spoon in her hand to her sneaker. She sighed at how ridiculous she was. Hiding behind a bowl because West Montgomery was coming up the path to the house? Heck yeah, she was. Annabel had been back in Blue Gulch less than twenty-four hours and already the one person she wanted to avoid was rapping on the door.

He had something in his hand, she noticed as she bolted up, another dollop of batter flying to the floor. Was that a checkbook? Maybe he wanted to wave his money around to secure a Saturday night reservation for Hurley's best table, the one that faced the Sweet Briar Mountain Range in the distance. Last night, Annabel's first at taking over as cook in the small restaurant's kitchen, Jillian Quisper, homecoming queen back in high school, had gotten engaged to PJ Renner right at that round table for two. Jillian had screamed for joy so loud that everyone in the kitchen had run out to make sure she wasn't choking on her plain green salad. It was no surprise that one of the wealthiest men in Blue Gulch would choose to propose in a small Western-style restaurant like Hurley's; most everyone in town had had their first date at Hurley's as teenagers. Parents knew Gram Hurley would keep an eye on kids. Plus, there was no better place to get country-fried steak, ribs or a pulled pork sandwich in the entire county. Hurley's Homestyle Kitchen meant something to just about everyone in town, homecoming queens included. Telling folks her intended had proposed on one knee at Hurley's over baby back ribs would get any gal "aws" from everyone, especially at the mountain-view table under the elegant little chandelier.

Annabel's experience with marriage proposals at that table was limited to old daydreams and nightly fantasies about West Montgomery on one knee—ha. As if West would propose the traditional way. He'd buy a plane and skywrite a proposal. He'd spell it out in rocks down by the clearing in front of the woods. He'd grab her hand, look her deeply in the eye, see everything she felt and whisk her away to Vegas for a quickie ceremony in the Elvis Presley wedding chapel, not that she'd ever get married without her gram or sisters in attendance.

And not that West Montgomery would ever propose to her.

Would anyone? Sometimes she thought her cooking skills *were* all she had going for her in the romance department. Way to a man's heart and all that. As if her ability to make a barbecue sauce to rival her gram's had gotten her anywhere but right where she was, standing in a kitchen.

West shielded his eyes from the bright April morning sunshine and squinted in the window. As he spotted her, surprise crossed his features; then he held up his hand with something of a nod.

Annabel gripped the wooden spoon, took a deep breath, ran her hands down the front of her apron, a mistake, since it was speckled with flour, and headed to the kitchen's back door. The restaurant was in the Hurley family home, an old apricot-colored Victorian that had seen better days.

He knocked again. What could he want?

Annabel Hurley, you are twenty-five years old. Open the door and find out!

So she did. The sight of him, six foot three, leanly muscular in worn jeans and a green chambray shirt, those intense brown eyes the color of driftwood, his thick, wavy hair so dark it was almost black, had her knees slightly buckling. He wore a black Stetson, which he tipped at her.

"Annabel," he said, unease clear. "I didn't know you were back in town." His gaze went to her sneaker, with the glob of batter, then to the spoon she held so tightly her knuckles were white.

She loosened her hold. And wondered if he even remembered their night—just a precious hour, if that—in the loft of the barn on his family's ranch. Given what he'd done the next day, she'd bet her meager savings he'd forgotten the minute she left that night. "Just got here yesterday."

He seemed distracted, as though there was something weighing on his mind. She knew that look of his well. She wanted to reach out and smooth the worry lines on his forehead the way she once had done, but she couldn't, of course. He took a deep breath, clearly bracing himself to make the expected conversation, to ask how long she was staying, if she was having a nice visit; West Montgomery wasn't one for small talk.

He glanced at his watch and said, "Is your grandmother here? I need to sign up for her cooking class that starts tomorrow." So much for pleasantries. For anything resembling regret for how he'd treated her.

Annabel couldn't help staring at him, her gaze going to the one dimple. The man was impossibly good-looking, so good-looking she almost missed what he said.

"You want to sign up for the cooking class?" she asked. West in a kitchen. She couldn't even imagine it. Her grandmother had been offering cooking classes every season in their big country kitchen for as long as Annabel could remember. When Annabel was in middle school, her older sister had pointed out that Gram had to start the cooking classes to make extra money because she'd taken in her three orphaned granddaughters. Annabel had started helping out in the kitchen from that day forward.

He glanced past her at the counter, where ingredients for Gram's Famed Country Biscuits and homemade apple butter were spread out. "Is there room in the class?" He held up the checkbook. "I'll pay double if it'll get me in."

Double? What was *that* about? "Actually we had to cancel the spring session. My gram's not well and is getting lots of tests done." At the thought of her beloved grandmother, Essie, collapsing in the kitchen, the weight of a pan of grits suddenly too heavy for the fit seventy-five year old, Annabel closed her eyes for a moment, worry and fear snaking their way inside. She should have been here. Instead she'd been hours away in Dallas, trying to make her life work—for seven years. She could feel the guilt flaming her cheeks and turned away.

He took off his hat and held it against his chest. "That's why you're back," he said quietly. "I'm sorry about your grandmother. A few months ago, I ran into her in the supermarket when I was buying a birthday cake for my daughter. I told her my attempt caved in on itself, and she told me to put the store cake back, that she'd bake one for me. I tried to tell her that wasn't necessary, but she insisted and asked what my daughter's favorite things were. The next morning she brought over a cake in the shape of a tree, decorated with green leaves, branches, crab apples and a climbing girl all set in icing. Lucy flipped. She still talks about her birthday cake."

That was Gram. Always helping, always going the extra mile. Annabel smiled at her grandmother's kindness, but at his little girl's name, her chest tightened. Though she'd only been back to Blue Gulch for holidays and birthdays, she'd once run into West's heavily pregnant wife at the grocery store and another time she'd seen West with a toddler on his shoulders at a parade, a little girl with huge hazel eyes and wisps of dark hair like her daddy's. Lucy must be six now.

She headed back to the counter and gave the biscuit batter a stir. "Why do you want to take a cooking class?" she asked to change the subject.

He stepped in and closed the door behind him, looking everywhere but at her. "I need to learn some basics. Omelets, fried chicken, maybe chicken salad with the leftovers for sandwiches. That kind of thing. And biscuits like your grandmother makes."

She noticed he didn't answer the question. "Your wife could teach you that, I'm sure," she said like an idiot, the face of Lorna Dunkin Montgomery pushing into her mind. Of all the beautiful young women in town, the guy of Annabel's dreams had fallen for the meanest, the ringleader of the group back in high school that had dubbed Annabel "Geekabel" and made her feel ashamed of her scrawny figure, frizzy reddish-brown hair and home-sewn clothes, and how foolish she'd been to even dare have a secret crush on a boy like West. Back then, Annabel had had exactly two conversations with West, both making clear that the maverick in the black leather jacket and combat boots, his hair slightly too long, was as complicated and kindhearted as he was absolutely gorgeous. But falling for Lorna? Marrying her? She'd never gotten that. And she'd never gotten over it either.

A few months after her…moment with West in his barn, she'd happened on the bride and groom coming out of the church, their families throwing rice. *He must have gotten her pregnant*, she remembered meanly thinking, *to marry her after just a few months of dating*. Gram had brought her tissues and homemade fudge brownie ice cream, and by the end of their conversation Essie Hurley had convinced Annabel to accept the scholarship she'd been offered to a culinary school in Dallas—her dream—rather than stay in town to help Gram with the restaurant. Maybe Annabel would come back to Blue Gulch; maybe she wouldn't, Gram had said. *Follow your heart, wherever it leads.* She'd wanted to come back home, cook for Hurley's Homestyle Kitchen, maybe add a bit of city to the menu here and there to bring in business from the fancy steak house that had opened a few doors down. But then she'd seen pregnant Lorna. Seen West with his little girl and couldn't imagine watching the man she loved with another woman, a child. And so she'd stayed in Dallas, where she didn't belong.

"Lorna was killed in a car accident a little over a year ago," West said, his gaze going to his watch.

Shame at how she'd remembered his late wife came over her. "I'm very sorry, West. For you and your daughter." Annabel had heard through her grandmother that West's parents had died from smoke inhalation in a fire not too long after she went to cooking school. He'd lost his brother, his parents, his wife. So much loss at such a young age.

He held up his checkbook. "I made it out to Essie already. I realize you probably don't have a lot of time between the restaurant and seeing to your grandmother, but maybe you could squeeze in a lesson or two?"

Why was it so important that he learn how to make an omelet and a chicken salad sandwich?

She *could* help him out. A quick look at the books late last night made it clear that Hurley's Homestyle Kitchen had been losing money left and right the past six months—probably when Gram's health started failing. Essie had kept it a secret from everyone, even Clementine, Annabel's younger sister, who worked as a waitress at the restaurant. Annabel could use the money to keep inventory up, at least. For a few days anyway. Again she wondered if her older sister, Georgia, would come home. A businesswoman in Houston, Georgia was sorely needed at the restaurant to run the office, manage the financials. But she hadn't responded to Clementine's or Annabel's calls for two days now.

"Hattie, Gram's assistant cook, could probably teach you," Annabel said, realizing that despite needing his three hundred dollars for the six-week course, she couldn't bear the thought of being alone with him in close quarters, reminded of the night they'd shared, how she'd almost given all of herself to him and how he'd taken up with Lorna Dunkin the next day.

The next day. All over each other on the flat-topped boulder near where she went to pick herbs every afternoon. *Their* rock. She'd seen them with her own eyes.

Annabel turned away for a moment, chastising herself for how much it still stung, still hurt.

"Please, Annabel. I'm desperate."

"Desperate to learn to make biscuits?" she snapped before she could catch herself. Seven years ago was seven years ago. *You're not eighteen and he's not nineteen. He's a widower, for Pete's sake. A single father. And for some reason, he* is *desperate to learn to make biscuits.*

He frowned as he stared at her. "Will you teach me to cook or not?" The hat went back on. "You can condense the class if you want, an hour a few times a week for two weeks, early in the morning before opening or after closing—whenever's convenient." He took a pen from his back pocket, filled out another check, and held it out to her. "A thousand dollars. Please, Annabel."

A thousand dollars? Oh, heck. That she couldn't turn down. *You'll get through it*, she told herself. *You'll show him how to roast a chicken and cut up potatoes and that'll be that. No big whoop.* She glanced at him, then began stirring the biscuit batter even though it had thickened too much and was a lost cause. "The restaurant is closed on Mondays, so we might as well take advantage of using the kitchen. Be here at six sharp tomorrow. I'll assume you don't have your own apron."

His shoulders relaxed and he handed her the check. "Actually I do. My daughter made it for me during craft time at her camp last summer. Her colorful handprints are all over it."

She felt for the little girl who'd lost her mother. Annabel knew what that was like.

"Normally I wouldn't take this," she said, tucking the check in the back pocket of her jeans. "But things have been slow around here for the past few months since Gram got sick and didn't tell anyone. We could use the money."

He nodded and turned to leave.

"You don't mind that you're not getting Gram as your cooking teacher?" she asked. *Have you thought about me once in all these years? Why did you call a halt to...things that night?*

She knew why—thought she did anyway. Because it had dawned on him that he was getting hot and heavy with Geekabel. She'd just happened to be in the right place at the right time. He'd been grief-stricken over his brother's death and out of his mind; she'd been there with whatever comfort he'd needed. Then he must have opened his eyes and seen a too-skinny, frizzy-haired girl he'd never even noticed before, realized he'd been about to make love to Geekabel, sent her home and taken up with sexy, stacked Lorna Dunkin, with her platinum blond hair and 32-D chest and high heels. Annabel doubted that West even remembered her at all.

He turned back and held her gaze so intensely she had to look away. "I still think about that chili con carne you made me the day my brother died. I've never forgotten how good it was or how it actually managed to distract me for a minute from my grief. And you were how old, barely eighteen?"

So he did remember. An image pushed into her mind, of finding him sitting atop that big rock near the field where her gram had always sent her to collect chickweed and henbit, his arms wrapped around his knees, his head down, his back shaking. West Montgomery, sobbing, his older brother, an army soldier, killed in Afghanistan.

He shifted, straightening his Stetson and digging his hands in pocket. "Anyway."

"Anyway," she said, unable to stop the memory of the way he'd held her seven years ago in the barn where he'd hidden out during most of the sympathy visits to his parents' house. He'd eaten the chili and they'd talked some, and she'd known he wanted to say thank you but couldn't speak, wanted comfort but couldn't ask for it, so he'd just hugged her tightly and held on for a full minute, Annabel gripping his shoulders. He'd kissed her then, her knees actually buckling from the surprise, the sensation, the dream, and he'd picked her up and laid her down on the blanket in the straw.

She shook herself out of the memory and thought

back to what he said, about her chili distracting him from his grief. Was that why he wanted to learn to cook? To help with his loss of his late wife? He didn't look sad. If anything, he looked...worried. He hadn't said he wanted to learn to cook. He said he *needed* to. There was a story there, she'd bet on it.

He pulled a tissue from the pocket of his leather jacket and leaned over, dabbing it at her cheek. "Batter," he said. "See you tomorrow at six."

Annabel watched him head back up the path and get into his silver pickup. What the heck had she just agreed to?

At five-thirty on Monday, West took a bite of the homemade chicken tenders he'd cooked for his daughter and shook his head. What the blast was he doing wrong? He'd followed the recipe he found online. Put chicken in beaten egg, coat with flour, then fry in oil in a pan. What was so hard? Why didn't it taste like the chicken he had last week at Hurley's? It didn't even come close to the chicken dinners Lorna had served, which, granted, were nuggets from a big bag in the freezer. He'd relied on frozen, takeout and hot dogs too often. No more. But proof that he needed a cooking teacher was on the plate in front of him. And his daughter.

He looked over at six-year-old Lucy sitting across from him at the dining room table in their ranch house, his heart clenching as always at how much he loved her, how beautiful she was, her dark ringlets bouncing on her narrow shoulders with every poke of her fork at the green beans she wasn't eating. She'd had four bites. According to Lucy's pediatrician at her last checkup, that was perfectly normal for a six-year-old. She'd eaten two bites of the baked potato, which wasn't quite soft enough, even though he'd followed an online recipe to the letter—wrap in foil and bake for fifty minutes at 425 degrees—and then added some extra butter to make up for it. She'd eaten two bites of chicken. And she'd taken one sniff of a green bean and snuck it under the table to an always-hungry Daisy, their beagle.

"One more bite of chicken?" he said to Lucy.

She smiled, the dimple that matched his popping out in her left cheek, her big, round hazel-green eyes, just like her mother's, darting to her lap. "Okay, Daddy."

He watched her pick up a piece of the chicken with her fingers and surreptitiously slide her hand under the table where he knew Daisy was waiting. "Lucy Montgomery," he chastised, but couldn't help the smile.

Hell, he didn't want to eat his tough, bland dinner either. He scooped up Lucy from the table and held her tight, her arms around his neck the best feeling in the world. "You be a good girl for Miss Letty. She's going to watch you while I'm at a cooking class."

Annabel Hurley came to mind, tall and curvy, with that porcelain skin and long, silky auburn hair. He could still remember wrapping his hands in that hair, the cocoa-butter scent of it, the feel of her soft skin. The sight of her shyly taking off her sweater in the barn loft, the lacy white bra driving him mad with desire for her. If he could go back in time seven years ago, he'd have handled that night differently, wouldn't have let things have gone that far, no matter how badly he'd wanted things to have gone much, much further. But not with Annabel Hurley. Then again, if he could go back, there'd be no Lucy. That wasn't anything he wanted to imagine.

"Will you learn to cook ice cream?" Lucy asked, slipping Daisy another bite of chicken. Lucy's favorite thing on earth—besides a tree to climb—was a hot-fudge sundae.

"I will," he said, a chill snaking up his spine as he remembered his last conversation with Raina Dunkin, Lucy's grandmother—and Lorna's mother.

No young child should be having a hot fudge sundae at eleven o'clock in the morning! Raina had screeched at him in her high-pitched Texas drawl two days ago. She'd barged in for "an impromptu visit to check on my grandchild," in her trademark silk pantsuit and heels, and didn't even say hello to Lucy before asking Lucy to hand over the bowl of ice cream and then dumping it in the sink.

Furious, West had told Lucy as calmly as he could to go play in her room while he talked to Nana. The moment the girl left the room, Raina had stabbed her manicured finger at him and said, *You listen to me, West. You'd better start taking proper care of your daughter or Landon and I will have no choice but to petition for custody. We've given you plenty of time to adjust to being a single father. But it's constant hot dogs and candy. And now it's ice cream before lunch, which I have no doubt will be a fast-food burger. And her hair. God, West. Brush the girl's hair. Put it in a ponytail. And throw out those damn raggedy green pants already!*

How he'd held his temper was beyond him. *First of all, it's* Saturday, he'd snapped. *She can have messy hair if she wants and wear her favorite pants. Second of all, I'm doing the best I can*, he'd added, anger—and shame—burning in his gut.

Your best isn't good enough, now, is it? she said. *And if you'd watch her more closely, she wouldn't have scrapes and marks all over her legs like some wild boy.*

West loved to watch his daughter race around the yard and the playground structure after Daisy, following the beagle down the slide. Yeah, Lucy landed badly sometimes, and there were scrapes and cuts and bruises. When they played hide-and-seek, he always knew he'd find her hiding in the crab apple tree, so high up that sometimes it scared him. But Lucy was happy and loved and cared for. He had the love part of fatherhood down pat; it was the rest he wasn't great at. He mangled meals and resorted to fast food or Hurley's too many times. And he had trouble with the knots in Lucy's hair, so he let the shoulder-length ringlets do their own thing, resulting in weird tufts that his sitter would fix if she could. Miss Letty was a great sitter, kind and patient, and lived just five minutes down the road at the next ranch, but she'd said she'd never been much of a cook and West had to leave meals for her to heat up for Lucy.

My disappointment of a daughter couldn't even beat an egg, Raina had continued, *but at least she had Lucy looking presentable in public. Get your act together, Weston Montgomery, or I will see you in court.* She'd turned and stalked to the front door.

So much for his temper. *Don't you* ever *refer to Lucy's mother as a disappointment again*, he'd said through gritted teeth at Raina's back, his anger reaching the boiling point.

His and Lorna's marriage hadn't been good, and Lorna had told him she was leaving permanently—

and leaving Lucy behind—just a day before the car accident that had taken her life. But preserving a good memory of Lorna for his daughter was important to West, and no one, especially not Raina's mother, who had a history of slinging cruelty, would disparage his child's mother.

Raina had rolled her eyes and stormed out and West had needed to do something physical to get his anger out, so he'd taken Lucy over to Miss Letty's for an hour and then ridden fence along his vast property, mending and hammering his frustration out.

West vs. Parents. Story of his life. Lorna's wealthy, powerful parents had never liked him. Not only had his family been from the wrong side of the tracks in Blue Gulch, but he was the Montgomery family's black sheep. He and his own parents had never gotten along well; they'd lost their golden boy and had been left with the troublemaker when West was nineteen. Back then, West could imagine his father wishing it had been West who'd been killed overseas in Afghanistan, and his mother responding: *As if West had it in him to fight for his country in the first place.*

They'd never said that, but they might as well have. And before he could even try to show them who he was, they'd hightailed it out of Blue Gulch to start fresh in Austin, where Garrett had always wanted to live; a way to honor him, West figured. And to get away from West and his pregnant girlfriend and the gossip in town. But just a few months in, a fire had broken out from faulty wiring, and West had buried his parents, everything in him numb. Lorna and the Dunkins hadn't had much patience for him and his grief, which had turned him even more inward.

His relationship with the Dunkins hadn't improved much over the years either; he'd gotten their "little girl" pregnant and stolen her dreams, they'd said, then trapped her on a ranch in a life she never wanted ten miles from town, where they lived in a huge Colonial.

He couldn't lose Lucy—and not to the Dunkins. He'd do whatever he had to keep her. Which meant learning to cook. He'd tried hiring a housekeeper after Lorna's death, but one woman had harshly scolded Lucy for leaving her toys out in the playroom and made elaborate meals that West had told her neither he nor Lucy wanted to eat, such as beef bourguignon. The next housekeeper forgot Lucy was allergic to soy and made her some inedible vegetable-fruit smoothie with soy milk, which landed Lucy in the emergency room with severe stomach pains and a strained visit from the Dunkins about his carelessness.

He would learn to cook.

Taking a class from a Hurley would kill two birds too. Everyone in town, including the Dunkins, liked Gram Hurley, respected her, which was saying something. Essie Hurley had never been wealthy, but she was wise and had been something of a grandmother to most everyone in Blue Gulch in some way or another. Essie had once saved Raina Dunkin from public embarrassment; Lorna had told West all about it when they first got married. Raina would likely back off from threatening to sue for custody once they found out Essie's granddaughter, with her fancy Dallas culinary school background, was giving him cooking lessons. If they didn't, well, West had taken over his parents' small cattle ranch and had turned it into a very prosperous operation; he had the money to hire a good lawyer, but the toll it would take on West, the distraction from work and from Lucy, would just about kill him.

He'd learn to cook. He'd figure out how to get the knots out of Lucy's hair, even if the detangler the clerk in Walgreens told him about was no match for the thick curls.

What he wouldn't do was let himself fall for Annabel—again. He was done with romance, done with relationships, done with disappointing people. And besides, things with Annabel just cut too deep in too many ways. Where she was concerned, there was too much he wanted to forget.

Anyway, after the way he'd treated Annabel seven years ago, he was surprised she hadn't hit him over the head with that wooden spoon she'd been gripping yesterday.

West heard Miss Letty's car arrive and took Lucy out to meet her, the fresh April air a relief from the smell of rubbery chicken.

Lucy bounded over to her sitter, a tall woman in her early fifties with a long gray braid, jeans and sneakers for Lucy's outdoor play, and a warm smile. "Miss Letty, come play house with Daisy. I'm the mother and Daisy is the daughter and you'll be the grandmother." Lucy turned to Daisy, who eyed her skeptically. "Okay, Daisy, I said only one treat after lunch."

Miss Letty smiled and followed after Lucy, who pulled her by the hand. "You go ahead," Letty said to West.

He hugged and kissed Lucy goodbye, told Letty he'd pay her extra if she'd clean up the dinner dishes, which got him a wink and a sure thing, and then got in his pickup. Time to learn how not to screw up fried eggs.

Chapter Two

Yesterday, when Gram was reminding Annabel of how the restaurant worked, Essie Hurley had made clear that Mondays were a real day off—no prep, no cleaning, no ordering supplies. In fact, family who lived in the Victorian were only allowed in the kitchen on Mondays to cook simple meals for themselves. So at five-thirty, Annabel was surprised to come down the back stairs into the kitchen and find her younger sister, Clementine, kneeling in front of the sink and meticulously cleaning the little red rooster cabinet knobs. Twenty-four-year-old Clementine wore gray yoga pants and a long pale pink T-shirt, her feet in orange flip-flops and her long dark hair in a high ponytail.

"Clem?" Annabel said, watching her sister dip a rag into a small bucket of cleaning solution and go over the rooster's tiny tail.

Clementine turned around and shot Annabel a tight smile. "I forgot to clean these last night," she said, moving on to the next cabinet knob. "Aren't they cute? Georgia sent them from Houston a few months ago." She smiled again and returned to work, scrubbing at the rooster's crown.

Something was wrong. Annabel had been gone for seven years, and she and Clementine had never been as close as Annabel had hoped, even when they'd lived under one roof, but she knew when Clementine was holding back. Maybe Clem was angry at her for staying away so long. For leaving the restaurant and Gram on her shoulders all these years. It was hard to tell with Clem. Clem was a "fine, everything's fine" kind of person, the sort who'd tell you "no worries!" with a bright smile and then go off alone to cry over something dreadful that had just happened to her, like when her birth mother had stood her up for their twice-a-year reunions, only to text an hour later to say something had come up. Annabel's parents had adopted Clementine when she was eight from a bad foster-care situation, and though Clem's birth mother was cagey and distant, Clementine had worked hard, often fruitlessly, to keep up some kind of relationship with the woman.

If Clem was cleaning cabinet pulls—and on a Monday—something had happened.

"Is everything okay with you?" Annabel asked.

"I'm fine. Just worried about Gram." She glanced back at Annabel. "I'm *fine*, really."

Annabel wished her sister would open to her. But Annabel knew she couldn't rush things. This morning she and Clementine had taken Gram to an appointment at the county hospital; three hours later, after testing and poking, they were sent home, Gram told to rest as much as possible until the test results came in. Clementine had been quiet on the ride to the hospital, quiet there, quiet on the way back.

Now she glanced at the big yellow clock on the wall above the stove. "I promised Mae Tucker I'd babysit the triplets tonight. See you around midnight." With that, Clementine bolted up, dumped out the bucket and stored it away, then dashed up the back stairs.

It'll take time to rebuild your relationship with Clem, Gram had said during lunch earlier. *Don't give up on her.*

Annabel wouldn't. Ever. She'd never give up on family.

And she'd never give up on Hurley's Homestyle Kitchen either. Since the restaurant wasn't doing well, it was up to Annabel to keep the kitchen going. Folks counted on Hurley's to be open Tuesday through Sundays for lunch and dinner, and Annabel didn't want to let her Gram down.

West Montgomery wants to learn how to cook, does he? Gram had said that afternoon, taking a nibble of the potato chowder Annabel had made her. *Teach him everything I taught you,* Essie had added. *The tips and secrets. The things you can't learn by a recipe alone. I know he hurt you, Annabel. But I've seen him around town with that little girl of his and it would melt the heart of Constance Brichard.* Constance Brichard was the grumpiest person in town, an elderly widow who was always threatening to sic her mean little Chihuahua on kids for making too much noise at the bus stop across the street from her house.

Which made things worse for Annabel. If West could

get Constance Brichard to crack a smile, what would he do to *her*?

Annabel put on her favorite yellow apron and glanced at the clock—ten minutes till West walked through the door, daughter-sized handprint apron on.

She pulled the list she'd made from her jeans pocket. *Breakfasts: cheese omelet, scrambled eggs, quiche Lorraine, French toast. Bacon. Biscuits with apple butter.* Tonight's cooking lesson would be about breakfast. Annabel was about to open the walk-in refrigerator for the eggs and milk and butter, then realized if West was paying her a thousand dollars to learn how to make an omelet and biscuits, he could probably use a tutorial about the ingredients themselves, what to buy, how to store them.

A rap sounded at the back door and Annabel glanced out the window. There he was, right on time. She held up a hand and went to the door, taking a deep breath before she opened it.

"Got my apron," he said, clutching it in one hand.

She smiled and held the door open for him, willing herself not to stare at him, not to look too closely at his handsome face or the way his broad shoulders filled the doorway. He wore a navy blue T-shirt and low-slung jeans, a brown belt with a bronc buckle. He'd filled out from the nineteen-year-old boy she'd known. He was tall then, but now he was muscular from years of ranch work. "Come on in."

He hung his hat on a peg by the door, then stood at the huge center island.

Speak, Annabel. She cleared her throat. "Since you said you want to learn the basics, I thought we'd start with breakfast—scrambled eggs, omelets, French toast, bacon."

"Lucy loves scrambled eggs and French toast, and I love bacon, so all that sounds great."

"So Lucy is six?" she asked. Six. It just occurred to her that in all this time, all these years, of course he hadn't given Annabel two thoughts. She'd been so focused on how he'd dropped her like a hot biscuit for sexy Lorna when she should have realized it had been fatherhood that wiped his memory of all that had come before. One hour in the hayloft in his parents' barn where they'd groped and kissed? How could that even register amid the birth of a baby, the first cold, the first steps, the first day of school? How could it register against daily life with sweet miracles in the form of a toothless smile or a child's pride at learning to read?

She'd been a dope to wonder these past seven years if he'd thought about her. Of course he hadn't.

But that hadn't stopped her from tossing and turning for hours last night, remembering how it had felt to be in his arms, to be kissed so passionately by him. At around three in the morning, she'd made herself promise she wouldn't be sucked back in by his face, by his incredible body, by his…story. He had a story seven years ago. She'd responded and had her heart broken and her life set on a path she hadn't expected. She'd left her home, left her gram and her younger sister and had lived in a kind of emptiness, of going through the motions.

He had a story now. She might not be able to stop herself from responding; he was standing in her kitchen, after all, awaiting her help. But she would respond only so much, only so far. She wouldn't let him get to her, wouldn't let him affect her, wouldn't let him *in*.

West nodded and slipped on his apron. "I can't believe it, but yeah, she's six. She's in first grade and something of a math whiz."

"That's something I'll never be," Annabel said. "Although I know my way around a measuring cup and my ounces and quarts and gallons." She eyed the clock. One minute after six. For a thousand dollars, he was expecting results, not chitchat. "So, I also thought I'd walk you through the ingredients. We're going to start with scrambled eggs." She went over to the counter and picked up a stack of papers she'd inserted into a folder. "I made you a folder of recipes," she said, handing it to him. "Find the one for scrambled eggs and bacon and tell me what we need."

He opened the folder and scanned it. "Got it." He held out a sheet and put the folder back on the counter. "Eggs, milk, butter, bacon."

She explained how the bacon would take longer to fry than the eggs needed to cook, so they should start with the bacon. She went over the different kinds of bacon to buy, how folks at Hurley's liked thick-cut the best, how long to keep it, how to store it, and he jotted down notes on the recipe, listening intently to everything she said. She showed him different kinds of pans, from sauté to cast iron. A few minutes later he had single-file bacon beginning to sizzle in the pan, tongs at the ready.

"While that's cooking, let's get the eggs ready." She told him how many eggs to use for him and his daughter, how to crack them so the shells wouldn't land in the bowl, how to beat the eggs and for how long, how some people like to add a little milk and he could try it both ways, with or without, but she liked it with. A little salt and pepper and he was ready to pour the beaten eggs in the fry pan on the next burner.

The smell of frying bacon made her mouth water and she realized she hadn't eaten much today. By the time he was slowly stirring the eggs in the pan, she was ravenous. She had him turn the heat off the eggs and drain the bacon on paper towels, then transfer everything to two plates. After instructing him to grab a small handful of cherries from the basket on the counter and add it to the plate, they sat down at the round table by the window.

"Depending on how hungry you are, you can add toast or biscuits too," she said. "Well, dig in."

He glanced at his plate, then forked a bite of eggs into his mouth. "I made this? It's pretty good." He leaned back as though relieved. She wanted to ask again why he was paying a thousand dollars to learn to make a few basics, but as she stole a glance at him while he popped a cherry into his mouth, that mouth she'd fantasized about for at least three years of high school before he'd ever kissed her, she could see the hard set of his jaw, something inscrutable in his eyes. He didn't want questions, didn't want to talk. He wanted to learn to cook and was paying good money for it.

Okay, then.

She dragged her gaze off him and took a bite of eggs, then tasted a piece of bacon. "It's better than good. It's absolutely delicious." Nerves made her ramble on about how he could get the best tasting eggs from the farm stands in town, rather than from the supermarket. He did a lot of nodding in response and said maybe he'd get some chickens of his own, that his daughter would love that.

Aware that their knees were awfully close and had brushed together more than once, Annabel couldn't take it and got up with the excuse that she could use some coffee.

"Ditto," he said. "Guess we were both hungry," he added, glancing at their empty plates. "I imagine you have your hands full, cooking for the restaurant and caring for your grandmother. I appreciate you taking me on."

As a student only.

"Well, we really need the money," she said pointedly, and he glanced at her. *Don't follow up that comment, don't qualify, just move on to French toast. He doesn't need to know your business, that he hurt you so badly you wouldn't help him if you didn't have to.* Which would be a lie. Of course she'd help him. But he didn't need to know Gram's business, how much trouble the restaurant was in. If only Georgia would call back. Talk about a math whiz. Georgia Hurley ran a company in Houston. She'd know how to get Hurley's back in the black.

A half hour later, on their second cup of coffee, they sat at the same spot, trying the French toast they'd made, the first bite with a sprinkle of cinnamon.

"Delicious," he said. "I wish I wasn't so full from all that bacon I ate."

She laughed. "Me too. But try a piece with cinnamon and a sprinkle of confectioners' sugar."

"Lucy will love this," he said, swiping a bite in some maple syrup—which she quickly explained was the real thing and worth every penny.

They moved on to a western omelet, with West slicing and dicing vegetables—mushroom, green and red peppers and onions. He stood beside her at the island, slicing the mushrooms a bit too thick.

"Thinner," she said, moving his hand on the knife a bit to the left. "The mushrooms will sauté quicker and won't be too chunky in the omelet."

He glanced at her hand on his, and pulled away slightly. "Got it," he said.

Annabel, you fool, she chastised herself, feeling like a total idiot. Hadn't Gram told her he had women throwing themselves at him since his wife had died? A gorgeous widower with a sweet little girl and a prosperous ranch brought out all kinds, Gram had said. Now he probably thought she was flirting. Grrr. Her cheeks flamed with embarrassment. Seven years in Dallas might have changed Annabel from that scrawny, frizzy-haired girl into a woman who knew her way around a little makeup and a blow dryer, but she was a jeans and T-shirt kind of gal and always would be and wore her long auburn hair in a low ponytail, tool of the trade. West wasn't really attracted to her seven years ago, and with a glamorous wife like Lorna, who'd worn push-up bras and high heels to the supermarket at ten in the morning, he wouldn't be attracted to her now. *Especially* now, when she smelled like bacon grease and cinnamon. Real sexy.

She just had a "duh" moment. His sudden interest in cooking was likely tied to his wife's recent passing. For the past year, he'd probably been responsible for feeding his daughter and maybe he'd burned a few breakfasts or bungled some dinners.

She moved to the other side of the counter. "You can slide those mushrooms and the onions in the pan," she said, showing him how to gently sauté them with a wooden spoon.

He nodded and glanced out the window as if all he really wanted to do was get out of here.

Unnerved and unsure what to do, what to say, Annabel thought about launching into a discussion of how to properly store vegetables, but she could see something was wrong, that she'd crossed a line. For touching him? Maybe she should remind him that *he'd* crossed a line, that he'd touched *her*—ran his hands over her bra, kissed a line down her stomach to the waistband of her jeans. And then dumped her without a damned word the next day.

It doesn't matter, she reminded herself, a hollow feeling opening in her stomach. It was a long time ago. A lifetime ago for him. *You're his cooking teacher, Annabel. That's it.*

"The Dunkins were in for dinner last night," she said to change the subject—the one in her head anyway.

He stirred the mushrooms, peppers and onions. And didn't respond. Interesting.

Raina and Landon Dunkin, Lucy's maternal grandparents, had left Clementine a huge tip too. Raina, a former Miss Texas contestant, had special ordered a mixed green salad, dressing on the side, with grilled chicken breast and just a bit of Hurley's famed Creole sauce. Landon, a nice enough but reserved man who'd done very well for himself in real estate, had the barbecue crawfish po'boy special, with its side of slaw and sweet potato fries. When Annabel had peered through the little round window on the kitchen door to see how busy the dining room was, she saw the Dunkins lingering over cappuccino, deep in quiet conversation.

"The restaurant sign could use some fresh paint," West suddenly said, gesturing out the window where the Hurley's Homestyle Kitchen sign, hanging from a post by the white picket fence, clearly needed some sprucing up. Hmm. Guess West wasn't interested in chatting about the Dunkins. Just bored by the small talk? She wasn't sure. "And the walkway needs work. There are a couple of loose stones. It's okay now, but in a few weeks they'll come loose enough that someone could trip and sue you for everything."

Annabel closed her eyes, a swirl of panic shooting up her spine. There was no money. Gram admitted yesterday that the restaurant was losing money every day. There was little in the account for repairs. With everyone knowing Essie was out of commission, Hurley's just wasn't the same. Clementine had suggested holding a fundraiser; after all, didn't everyone love Hurley's? The place was a community treasure. But Gram had shot down that idea and had called it charity. *You're just as good a cook as I am, better probably*, Gram had said this afternoon as she finished her potato chowder. *There's something special in your cooking. Folks just have to have the chance to know that. Give it time.*

"I'll take care of it," Annabel said to West, then instructed him to turn the heat off the vegetables. "We have some paint in the basement, I think. And I can probably watch a YouTube video on re-whatevering the stones on the path." She made a mental note to check on the paint and look up "whatevering" stones.

West eyed her, took a sip of his coffee and said, "It'll take me ten minutes to do both myself. *I'll* take care of it." She watched him transfer the vegetables onto the cheese she'd had him sprinkle on the eggs, then showed him to carefully flip half the omelet over.

She wanted to tell him to forget about it, but she wasn't above accepting help when she really needed it. "I'd appreciate that, West. Thanks."

"Least I can do," he said, plating the omelet. He cut it in two, then slid half onto another plate, added another handful of cherries and brought both plates to the table. He was getting pretty good at this. "Really. You have no idea."

So tell me, she wanted to shout.

They sat down at the table and he took a couple of bites of the omelet. "This is delicious," he said. "I really hope I can do this myself when you're not standing beside me. You're a good teacher, Annabel." He took a long slug of his coffee, finishing it, then got up. "How's tomorrow after the restaurant closes for the lunch lesson? Could you come to the ranch? My daughter will be spending the night at her grandparents' house, so I'll have extra time and I like the idea of learning to cook onsite. But if it's too late, I can come here in the morning."

Alone with him at his house. At night. She cleared her throat. "Tomorrow after closing will be fine," she said. "I'll be over by nine-thirty. We close at nine, but I'll need to help clean up."

He nodded, took his Stetson off the coat hook by the door and left, twenty different thoughts scrambling around Annabel's head. But the one that stood out was about how she'd feel being over at the Montgomery Ranch. For the second time.

Tuesday afternoon, just an hour after Lucy had come racing off the school bus, waving her "sight words" quiz

with *100%* and a smiley face at the top, West rushed
Lucy to Doc McTuft's office, cursing himself with what
was left of his breath. They'd been in the backyard,
Lucy on the low sturdy branch of her favorite climbing
tree, calling out words and spelling them, West nailing
on the piece of wood for the roof of the new dollhouse
he promised to make for her. One minute Lucy had been
saying, "Daddy, look how high I am—am, *A M*!"—and
she'd been so high that he called himself an idiot for
not watching more closely—and the next, she let out a
high-pitched yelp and was on the ground.

Doc McTufts had assured him that Lucy was fine,
no broken bones, and that the doc herself had fallen
out of plenty of trees as a kid and lived to tell the tale
to worried parents all over town. But of course, as they
were settling up at the reception desk, who was giving
him the stink eye but the Dunkins' next-door neigh-
bor, sitting with pursed lips next to her daughter and
grandbaby. As West drove home, Lucy in her car seat
in the back with her superhero coloring book, he figured the woman had already called Raina to let her
know her poor granddaughter had almost been injured
and had left the doc's office with a big bandage over a
nasty scrape.

Lucy was all right. That was what mattered. But he
would keep a better eye on her when she was climbing.

"Daddy, can we have ice cream for dinner?" Lucy
asked.

"How about your second favorite for dinner and ice
cream for dessert?" he asked, smiling at her in the rearview mirror.

"French toast with strawberries for the mouth and
blueberries for the eyes?"

"Sounds good to me," he said, feeling pretty confident about his French toast after yesterday's cooking lesson. Plus, hadn't Annabel said that she'd often eaten breakfast for dinner in Dallas when she was feeling low or missed her family? Comfort food. The very reason he ate at Hurley's so often.

He'd lain awake for hours last night, thinking about the cooking lesson. Annabel was so beautiful with that silky dark red hair caught in the ponytail, her pale, porcelainlike skin free of makeup, her long, lush body in low-slung jeans rolled up at the ankles and a loose white button down shirt tucked in. Her uniform, she'd called it. He called it sexy. She was like summertime, like sunshine, and her nearness, the scent of her, the sight of the swell of her breasts against the cotton shirt, the curve of her hip…it had been all he could do not to grab her against the wall and kiss her, memories of their time in the barn hitting him hard, as he'd shaken confectioners' sugar on French toast, slid peppers around in the pan.

And then she'd touched him, her soft hand, her skin electrifying his with the most casual of gestures, moving his hand over on the knife. Her touch had sent a shock through him and brought him back to the barn to forty-five minutes when he thought he'd found his future, when he thought everything made sense.

Until it didn't.

Back then West had been going nowhere fast. Annabel would have joined him there if he'd let something happen between them. After he and Annabel had almost gone too far in the barn, he forced himself to stop for her sake and said he'd better get back to the house. She'd gotten a funny look on her face, and he'd wanted to ask her if she was okay, to get a handle on why she seemed upset, but she seemed in a hurry to get away. From him. Maybe she'd just meant to pay her condolences, nice enough to bring him his favorite chili con carne that he always ordered to go after school, and he'd practically ripped her clothes off. *Jerk*. Maybe she was just being nice and he'd taken things too far, like always.

So then they'd gone back to the house so she could say goodbye to his parents, but his parents were standing outside, his mother crying, his father's arm over her shoulder, and they'd seen West and Annabel come out of the barn. He held back a bit and it was too late to tell Annabel she had a bit of hay in her hair. He saw his mother stare at the hay, then glance at him, disapproval turning her grief-stricken eyes cold. West doing the wrong thing again—fooling around with a girl in the barn while friends and neighbors came to pay their respects. That wasn't how it was, but it was how it had looked to his parents. West was sure of it.

Annabel had told his parents how sorry she was for their loss, glanced at West with such sorrow, then she'd gotten on her bike and raced away. Later that night, after the last of the relatives had left, West had come downstairs for a cold drink when he overheard his mother crying again and his father comforting her. The sound of his mother crying was like a slam in his gut, and West had stood there, frozen, his head hung, wishing he could go in and say the right thing, but he'd known, he'd always known, that he wasn't "living up to their expectations" and he'd be no comfort, that the wrong Montgomery brother was gone. Then he'd heard his mother say Annabel's name and he strained to hear.

Did you see West and Annabel come out of the barn together? his mother was saying. *She had hay in her*

*hair. Hopefully her grandmother will have the sense to
tell Annabel to stay away from West. I hear she has a
scholarship to culinary school in Dallas. I'd hate for
her to give up her future.*

West had gone rigid. He'd waited for his father's response, for some kind of defense, but his dad had said,
She won't give that up to stay in Blue Gulch.

*Plenty of girls give up their dreams for handsome
boys they're in love with,* his mother had said. *Annabel
has her whole life ahead of her, and West will be here,
doing what? Odd jobs. New girlfriend every weekend.
I love West, but he's...who he is.*

Who he is... His heart in his throat, he'd crept
back upstairs, lying awake for a long, long time, tears
streaming down his face. He'd lost his brother. His parents thought he was nothing. And now he had to lose
Annabel—to save her...from himself. His mother was
right. Annabel was a good girl, straight A's, helped out
her grandmother by working in the family restaurant
every day after school as a cook's assistant and sometimes as a waitress when someone called in sick. And
West was the troublemaker in the black leather jacket,
calls to his parents from the principal about fights he
got into with jerk jocks who thought they could say
anything they wanted about anyone. And yeah, since
barely graduating, he worked for room and board at a
big spread on the outskirts of town, thinking he might
want to be a rancher, breed cattle, raise horses. His
dad was a mechanic who'd tried his hand at starting a
small ranch on their property and hadn't done well, so
his father had figured West would fail at that life too.
But West wasn't like Garrett, who'd joined the military

and planned to become a police officer, a trajectory his parents could be proud of.

Back then he'd lain awake for hours, vowing to avoid Annabel Hurley so that he wouldn't screw up her life. In the barn, she'd taken off her sweater, let him touch her breasts in the lacy white bra, and kissed him deeper and deeper, driving him wild until he'd stopped things, afraid to go too far and take advantage of the situation.

So yeah, she liked him. That had been clear. Liked him enough to give up her scholarship and Dallas? Maybe. So he'd made the decision to avoid her from that moment on, let her go have her great life with a better guy than him.

And when Lorna Dunkin had told him the next day that she knew exactly how to make him forget his grief for a little while, looking him up and down and whispering in his ear, he took her to the flat-topped boulder where he often saw Annabel picking herbs for her grandmother, and he let Lorna help him forget everything— losing his brother, his parents' disappointment in him, his disappointment in himself and giving up Annabel for her own damned good. At some point, he'd heard the crack of a twig and he knew it was her, knew that she saw, and the footsteps running away let him know he'd achieved his goal.

Some damned victory.

Except about six weeks later, Lorna had shown him a white stick that looked like a thermometer with a pink plus sign in a tiny window and said she wanted a big wedding.

Lucy had made everything he'd given up worth it. But those times when he'd be stacking hay or training a horse, he'd think of Annabel's beautiful face, those round dark brown eyes, full of trust, of feeling, and he'd feel like the scum of the earth. He'd hurt her, no doubt. But hadn't she gone off to Dallas to the fancy cooking school? Hadn't he stepped out of her way? He'd heard she had a condo in a swanky apartment building near Reunion Tower. That she was a chef at a Michelin-starred American fusion restaurant, whatever that meant. She probably had a serious boyfriend in a fancy suit.

With Lucy lying on her stomach on the living room rug with her coloring book, Daisy half snoozing nearby, West opened the folder of recipes Annabel had given him. Breakfast was written in red marker on the tab in her neat script. He found the one for French toast, and set to work, cracking eggs, melting butter in the pan, getting out the bread. Soon enough he had four slices of French toast cooking, eyeholes cut out for blueberries and a mouth cut out for strawberry slices for Lucy's portion. Smelled pretty darned good too.

He thought about all those women coming by, in the first couple of months after Lorna died, with casseroles and offers to cook for him. There'd been innuendo and flat-out invitations. More than a few times he'd taken up those invitations, needing to forget, to be taken out of himself. And more than a few times he'd failed Lucy. One time he'd been in a woman's bed when he was supposed to pick up Lucy early from school for a dentist appointment, but the woman had made him forget himself so well he forgot his own daughter. Another time Lucy had been calling him over and over on the phone from Lorna's parents' house, where she was sleeping over, to tell him she lost a tooth, her first, but he'd shut the ringer so no one could interrupt him while a stranger with big breasts was naked beside him.

The next morning, the look of absolute disdain and disappointment on Raina Dunkin's face had said it all. *A father, especially a* widowed father*, needs to be reachable at all times, West,* she'd practically spit at him. But it was the look on Lucy's face, with one of her bottom front teeth gone, the *where were you, Daddy? I tried to call you like one million times* that had made him vow that was it. No more women. No more whiskey. No more hiding from his life. He'd focus on his daughter.

So beautiful women with long red hair and dark brown eyes, who made him want to rip off their loose jeans and white button-down shirts, women like Annabel Hurley, just couldn't go around casually touching his hand while slicing mushrooms.

"Daddy, I think Daisy ate my silver crayon," Lucy called from the living room. "She's choking!"

West rushed into the living room, where Daisy was sputtering a bit, trying to get something out of her mouth and pushing on her teeth with her paw.

"Daddy, is Daisy okay?" Lucy asked, hazel eyes worried.

"Well, let's see if we can help her," he said, kneeling beside Daisy and opening the beagle's mouth, where half a crayon was wedged in her back teeth. "Daisy, that couldn't possibly have tasted good," he said, shaking his head and trying to pop up the flattened, bitten crayon. Finally out it came. As the smell of something burning wafted into the living room, Daisy stood up and spit out the other half of the crayon.

Damn it, the French toast! It would be burned to a crisp by now.

The doorbell rang just as West was rushing back into the kitchen, so he quickly shut off the burner, then noticed he'd left the bag of bread too close to the burner; part of it started to cinder. He threw that in the sink and stood there for a moment, hands braced on the counter, wishing his headache away.

"Daddy, the doorbell rang again," Lucy called out just as the smoke alarm started blaring.

"Lucy, it's Nana and Pop-Pop," he heard Raina's shrill voice call out. "Come open the door, sweetheart."

Oh, hell.

He quickly tried to fan the smoke from the alarm with a magazine, then hurried into the living room, where Raina and Landon glared at him.

"*What* is that burning smell?" Raina said, barreling in and heading for the kitchen. West could hear her shoving up the kitchen window, and in a few moments, the alarm stopped its beeping. Raina was back in the living room in seconds, holding the charred bag of bread. "Blackened bread is in a pan on the stove. This burned bag was in the sink, and the kitchen is all smoky, which can seriously hurt developing lungs. God, West."

"We had a mergency with Daisy because she ate my crayon," Lucy said, holding up the flattened sliver for her nana.

"Even the dog isn't safe in this house," Landon said, shaking his silver-gray head at West as he took the crayon from Lucy. "I'll make sure this ends up in the garbage so there isn't another 'mergency.'"

"I heard Lucy was at the doctor today," Raina said as she went over to Lucy to examine her leg. She peeled back the bandage and added her own head shake at the nasty cut. He watched Raina's gaze take in Lucy's torn purple leggings, the scrape on her arm, the knot clumping together a cluster of ringlets on the left side of her head, the dirt smudge on her cheek.

"I fell out of the tree today," Lucy said proudly, sticking out her injured leg.

"Oh, I can see that," Raina said, shooting a death stare at West. "Lucy, can you go play in your room?" she added through gritted teeth. "Grandpa and I need to talk to your father."

When Lucy left, Raina lowered her voice. "You leave me no choice, West. We've given you a year to get your act together. But you're unfit to parent Lucy alone. Landon and I will be filing for custody. This was the final straw." She held up a hand. "Don't bother to defend yourself," she said, and then they swept out.

West dropped down on the sofa, his head in his hands. *No one* was taking his daughter away from him. But how would he fight the Dunkins when a lot of circumstantial evidence said he wasn't exactly father of the year?

"Daddy, is the French toast ready? I'm starving," Lucy said as she burst out of her room. "Hey, where's Nana and Pop-Pop?" she asked, looking around.

Keep it together for Lucy, he ordered himself. *The Dunkins aren't taking your girl away. They can't.* He'd figure it out, he'd fight them, he'd...do whatever he had to do.

He sucked in a breath and let it out. "They had to get home. You know what, Lucy? Even Daisy wouldn't eat the burned French toast. How about dinner at Hurley's, just the two of us? Go wash your hands, sweetcakes."

As Lucy grinned and ran to wash up, West felt a slow snake of cold fear slither up his spine. Could the Dunkins prove he was unfit? He was a better father now than he was in the terrible first month after Lorna's death, when Lucy didn't quite understand where her mother was, but had two sets of doting grandparents. He'd let them do what he should have done—been there for his daughter. Then his parents moved away…and he'd lost them too—permanently. Instead of focusing on being a good dad to Lucy, he'd drank too much and spent too many nights with women, trying to make himself forget who and what he was. A man very much alone who had no idea how to be a good father.

He would not lose his daughter. No matter what he had to do.

Chapter Three

According to Clementine, at 6:30 p.m., prime dinnertime, every table at Hurley's Homestyle Kitchen should be taken, a line of folks waiting on the porch, where waiters would circulate with complimentary sweet tea and Gram's beloved smoked and spiced nuts. Now, at that exact hour, she and Clementine glanced around the dining room, Annabel worrying her lower lip and Clementine furious.

"This is how everyone supports Gram after fifty years? By staying home because she's ill and not doing the cooking?" Clementine asked, shaking her head.

"Well, Gram is Gram," Annabel said, watching through the back window as Olivia Piedmont and her husband craned their necks into the kitchen, saw Gram's assistant cook, Hattie, and her helper, Harold, and then pointed across the street to the Sau Lin's Chinese Noodle Shop. Not that Annabel wanted to take business away from Sau Lin's, which had been around a long time too, but Hattie had been cooking beside Gram for thirty years. And now here was Annabel, who'd learned to shred chicken and create a killer barbecue sauce by the time she was eight.

Five of the fifteen tables were taken. Five. And when Lindy, one of the waitresses, rolled out the dessert cart to tables two and four, only one person ordered a piece of the special chocolate fudge pie.

Every day that continued like this meant Hurley's Homestyle Kitchen would be in big trouble within two months. Tonight, after the cooking lesson, Annabel would spend some time coming up with an idea to bring in business. That was the constant talk at staff meetings at the three restaurants where Annabel had worked in Dallas—everything was about retaining patrons and bringing in new ones. But here in Blue Gulch, there wasn't exactly the same competition to study as there had been in Dallas. If people quit Hurley's because the best cook in the world was no longer doing the cooking, all the initiative in Texas wouldn't help.

Annabel would just have to up her game and try, try, try. A menu board listing the delectable specials outside. A Facebook page with photos that would have mouths watering. A new children's corner with games and toys and mats and maybe Annabel could hire a sitter for the section. She felt a little better already.

Except when Danielle Tolliver and her Tuesday night book club meeting got up to leave, Annabel overheard Danielle whisper to one of the women that the chicken-fried steak's gravy just wasn't the same.

Annabel had made that gravy. Maybe it had too

much Dallas in it, not enough Blue Gulch. She had to remember she was home now, that people like old-fashioned, good food, not newfangled spices in thinner sauce. No one was counting fat grams at Hurley's.

Deep breath taken, Annabel was about to head back into the kitchen when she froze, her heart speeding up, unable to take her eyes off the man who'd just walked through the door of the restaurant. West Montgomery. He held his little girl's hand. Clementine walked over with a smile and led them to a table overlooking the hill out back with its wildflowers.

Annabel should go over and say hello and thank him—he must have gotten up early and silently gone to work on the Hurley's Homestyle Kitchen sign, because the sign was freshly painted and the loose cobblestones fixed. A man of his word. Instead she waved, then scurried into the kitchen, her reaction to the sight of West, the gorgeousness of him, scaring the bejesus out of her.

Hattie was on the grill, her assistant, elderly Harold, on sides and salads. Annabel was helping both of them and in charge of sauces and kitchen management, and was trying her best to become a better baker. When Clementine came with the Montgomery order—roast beef po'boy for West and a children's mac and cheese for Lucy—Hattie was so busy with a special-ordered fish that Annabel took care of West's and Lucy's orders.

She was making their dinner. Which felt very... domestic. A fantasy poked in her head about what it would be like to live with West and Lucy. A thought she forced out of her head. West had hurt her so bad seven years ago that she wasn't sure she'd ever let herself fall in love again. Granted, he'd been a grieving mess that night and she shouldn't blame him too harshly, but she couldn't help it. He'd put a halt to things with her, then had been doing the same things with Lorna Dunkin out in the open, not caring if she saw them or not.

That was who West was; she had to remember that. People always showed you who they were loud and clear, right? That was what Gram always said. So why did West not seem like a thoughtless jerk? She peered through the little window on the door to the dining room and caught West helping Lucy color on her children's place mat. That wasn't a sign of a jerk.

She thought of herself at eighteen, alone and lonely and out of her element in Dallas, trying so hard to fit in and eventually succeeding while feeling…empty. Now she was back home where she belonged and she wasn't about to let herself want West Montgomery again. No matter how many cobblestones he fixed or how many times he played thumb war with his daughter at Annabel's favorite table in Hurley's. No matter how much she wanted to join them.

The moment she peered out the window into the dining room, West happened to see her and waved her over. She was covered in gravy stains and had flour in her hair, but such was the life of a cook.

She weaved her way through the tables, smiling at the Henry family, catching one of the waiters' eyes to refill water on table three, and stopped in front of West and his daughter's table.

She kneeled down beside Lucy. "Hi, I'm Annabel Hurley. I'm one of the cooks here. I hope you liked your macaroni and cheese." Considering there was only a scrape of cheese left in the bowl, she felt safe putting the girl on the spot.

"It was really good," Lucy said. "We were going to

have French toast, but it burned because Daisy ate my crayon."

"Long story," West said, ruffling his daughter's hair. "Want to split a piece of chocolate layer cake?" he asked Lucy. "That looks amazing," he added, upping his chin at the delectable dessert heading over to another table.

"Yes!" Lucy said. "With whipped cream and a cherry on top."

"She wants everything to be like a sundae," West pointed out.

Annabel smiled at the adorable girl. "How would you like to come into the kitchen and help me make your sundae cake?"

The girl slid out of her chair. "Yes!"

Lucy slid her hand into hers, the sweet gesture poking at her heart. West glanced at their hands and smiled at Annabel, following them into the kitchen.

After introductions to Hattie and Harold, Annabel led Lucy to the dessert table, holding three chocolate layer cakes, four kinds of pie and a big plate of butter cookies. Annabel sliced a piece of cake, then brought Lucy over to the walk-in refrigerator, where the girl spun around with her mouth open.

"I'm in a refrigerator!" she exclaimed.

Annabel laughed and pointed out the tub of whipped cream, which she put in Lucy's outstretched hands, and then they headed back to the dessert table. Annabel handed her a scoop, and Lucy dug in and released a perfect mound of whipped cream on the cake. "Now for the cherry so it's a real cake sundae." Annabel held out a basket of cherries.

Lucy grinned and grabbed one by the stem, then carefully, her little pink tongue sticking out in concentration, placed it just so in the center of the whipped cream.

"We'd better let Ms. Hurley get back to work," West said, mouthing a thank-you to Annabel. "What do you say, sweetheart?"

"Thank you, Ms. Hurley," Lucy said.

Annabel kneeled down and smiled at her. "You can call me Annabel. And you're very welcome. Enjoy your cake, but remember to save some for your dad."

Tongue sticking out in concentration again, Lucy carefully carried the plate in two hands out of the kitchen to her table.

West looked at Annabel for a long moment, then seemed to realize he had an audience—Hattie and her assistant, Harold—and cleared his throat. "See you later at my place," he said before disappearing through the door. He was back in a heartbeat. "For the cooking lesson," he added, throwing a glance at Hattie and Harold.

Hattie could barely contain her big laugh while Harold smiled down at the potato chowder he was ladling into a bowl.

Annabel felt her cheeks warm but couldn't help the chuckle. Yet as she thought about being alone with West Montgomery in his house, in his kitchen, standing shoulder to shoulder at the counter, the chuckle was replaced by honest-to-goodness fear.

How did you stop yourself from falling for someone you'd never gotten over to begin with?

When the last table at Hurley's was cleared and the Open sign on the front door turned over, Annabel headed into the kitchen and cleaned up her station, the gloppy congealed lumps of white gravy that had fallen to the floor a particular pain in the neck. She was about to start on Hattie's grill section when Clementine took the heavy-duty sponge out of her hand.

"I know West Montgomery is waiting on you at his house, so go ahead. I'll take care of the cleanup."

Annabel squeezed her sister's hand in thanks. "That's okay. You were on your feet all night, just like I was. I'll do it."

"Go ahead," Clementine said, glancing at the clock at the wall—it was just past 9:00 p.m. "I don't have a hunky guy waiting for private cooking lessons." Clementine stared out the window for a long moment, her expression changing, and again, Annabel wondered what was up with her private younger sister.

"Clem, is everything okay? You can talk to me. You know that."

"I'm okay, I promise. Just got some stuff on my mind that a good round of cleaning will help me work out. Go." She pointed at the door. "Oh, wait. Maybe go after you wash the barbecue sauce out of your hair. And there's a small piece of fried chicken on your shoe."

Annabel hugged her sister—tight. She loved Clementine to pieces, but getting her to open up was like yanking teeth.

"I tried Georgia again on my break earlier," Clementine said, "but I got her voice mail, as usual. I know she left the message saying she couldn't come home just yet and was sorry, but what could be keeping her in Houston? What could be more important than Gram and Hurley's?"

"Something must be going on," Annabel said. She and Clementine had spent the past two nights trying to think of what that could be, but they were at a loss. The past few months, Georgia, a vice president of some fancy company, had been keeping to herself, checking in now and then with either Gram, Annabel or Clementine by phone or text and saying very little about her life. But not to come home now? Georgia was smart and strong, so Annabel had assured Clementine and their grandmother that Georgia must have a good reason for staying away and they'd just have to trust in her that she was doing the right thing for herself, even if it didn't make sense to family back home.

Trying to shift her worried thoughts from her older sister to the lunch recipes Annabel had made copies of and put in a folder for tonight's cooking lesson, Annabel headed upstairs to the third floor where the huge attic had long ago been turned into a bedroom for the three orphaned granddaughters Gram had taken in. Back then Essie Hurley had had the sections of the room painted in their favorite colors: lavender for Annabel, lemon yellow for Georgia and periwinkle blue for Clementine. Annabel's pale purple area with its white accents and fluffy pink blanket was just as she'd left it at eighteen. She picked up the photo of her parents, her beautiful mother and handsome, tall father, then another of the six Hurleys, Gram included, and took a deep breath. She stared at sixteen-year-old Georgia with her long sunlit brown hair and green eyes and hoped she was okay, wherever she was, whatever she was doing. Then she realized she had only twenty minutes to get to West's house. She stripped off her kitchen clothes, pulled on her old terry robe and took a quick, hot shower, her mind going to being in West's house, alone with him.

* * *

Annabel drove the ten miles out to West's ranch, the long paved drive lined with trees. The house came into view, and Annabel was surprised at how different the place was now. Instead of the run-down small home with peeling gray shingles that she remembered, the sprawling house was gleaming white in perfect condition with glossy black shutters and a red door, a wrought-iron weather vane with a rooster on the roof. A herd of cattle grazed in a dark pasture and another bunch was lined up in corrals, eating hay. Two geese waddled around, not bothered in the slightest by a big orange barn cat chasing a leaf in the evening breeze. West's silver pickup was along the side of the house, and by the front door was a red bike with training wheels and a three-wheeled silver scooter. The porch light illuminated the well-kept front yard and Annabel could see the long circular loop West had smoothed out for his daughter to ride. A tire swing with purple and white polka dots was tied on a big old oak, and nearby was a child-sized table and chairs, two big stuffed animals on the chairs and a tea set on the table.

Annabel's heart squeezed. She wondered if she'd ever have a little girl of her own. Over the past seven years she'd had only two relationships and both had failed miserably. Neither man had felt like…home, felt comfortable. But she'd tried, dating one for a month before he'd told her if they weren't going to have sex he'd have to move on. He'd moved on. The next man, a fellow chef, had smooth-talked his way into Annabel finally losing her virginity, but it turned out he'd been working his way through the female staff at the restaurant they both worked at, and she'd been the one to move on, to a new workplace but not a new relationship. She'd decided to avoid relationships, hoping maybe one day the right guy would cross her path and she'd know it and not have to force it, not have to try so damned hard.

Four years. Four years since she'd been kissed. Touched. Held. Four years of thinking back to that night in the hayloft with West, no one ever coming close to making her feel the way she had that night. In love. And as though she were on fire. As though she were beautiful and sexy. As though everything that made Annabel Hurley who she was blossomed brighter. She'd felt more herself that night with West, that hour, than she ever had before or since. Getting over his betrayal, the heartbreak, throwing herself into two bad relationships with men who didn't really care about her...she was better off alone, spending her evenings perfecting Gram's recipes and thinking up business initiatives for Hurley's. She would not let herself be drawn in by West, no matter how much her mind, heart and soul wanted him. He'd broken her once. That wasn't going to happen again. Her grandmother needed her—depended on her, especially now that Georgia was God knew where.

Keep your head, she ordered herself, straightening her purposely unsexy ponytail, smoothing her purposely unsexy long-sleeved yellow T-shirt, tucked into purposely unsexy on-the-loose-side old jeans. She picked up her lunch-recipes folder and the bag of groceries she'd shopped for on her lunch break and headed up the steps to the porch. She forced herself not to glance over to the right just past the house at the barn, now a traditional red, where she and West had spent an unforgettable hour.

She took a deep breath and rang the bell.

Seconds later, there he was, his expression serious as he ushered her inside, taking the bag of groceries. Before she could ask him if everything was okay, he headed toward the kitchen. She followed him through the living room, liking the two big red comfy-looking sofas, lots of throw pillows, a plush area rug, an enormous round wooden coffee table piled with kids' books and action figures and a furry dog bed on which a beagle eyed her.

"Daisy's not much of a watchdog," West said as he led the way into the kitchen, the walls a warm yellow, the wooden cabinetry white and appliances stainless steel. He put the bag of groceries on the island in the center of the room, and Annabel placed the folder next to it, then looked over at West, who was holding up a bottle of red wine. She nodded and he poured two glasses.

"The more you can pack into tonight's lesson, the better," he said, handing her a glass.

She took the wine, wishing she could read his mind. Something was clearly bothering him. "Are you ever going to tell me why it's worth one thousand bucks to make a chicken salad sandwich?"

He leaned back against the refrigerator, covered in his daughter's paintings and school notices and quizzes, and took a long drink of his wine. "That's complicated."

Chicken salad was complicated? She waited for him to elaborate, but he didn't. "Okay," she said. "So let's get started." She dug into the grocery bag, taking out a rotisserie chicken. "At our dinner lesson, I'll teach you how to roast a chicken, using the leftovers for chicken salad sandwiches the next day. But for now we'll use a preroasted chicken. Rotisserie chickens are great when you're in a hurry—"

He put his wine down and came over, standing so close she could smell his shampoo. He stared at the chicken. She realized he'd been a million miles away and had just clicked back to her. "I admit I buy those a few times a week. Quick and easy."

"That's fine," she said, for a moment overwhelmed by his nearness, by his muscled forearm, his hand in his pocket. Annabel was tall, almost five foot nine, but West towered over her at six-three.

To stop focusing on his face, his body, the clean scent of him, she launched into a lecture about how long to keep a roast chicken in the fridge, then ticked off on her fingers the various lunches he could make from it.

"Aside from chicken salad, there's tacos, stir-fry, po'boys, cold or hot chicken sandwiches and—" She stopped, realizing that he was staring out the window... at nothing she could see. He was definitely preoccupied. His gaze moved to the sink, where Annabel could see a cup with cartoon monkeys on it. "West? Are you all right?"

He paced to the window, then over to the refrigerator, where he stared at the photographs and watercolors his daughter had painted. Then he titled his head back and closed his eyes for a second.

Whatever was complicated about chicken salad was tearing West apart.

"This is what it'll feel like," he finally said. He paced the length of the kitchen. "This goddamned silence is what it'll be like if they take her away from me. The lack of her, the weird quiet that comes from not hearing her voice, her saying 'Daddy, look,' every two minutes."

He grabbed an apple from a basket on the island and hurled it into the sink so hard it bounced back and landed on the floor. Daisy came over and sniffed it, then stared up at West. He kneeled down beside the dog and buried his face in her brown bristly fur, picking up the apple and tossing it in the trash. "Damn it, damn it, damn it."

Annabel froze, then kneeled down across from him and put her hand on his shoulder. "If who takes who away from you? Are you talking about your daughter?"

He stood up and walked across the kitchen, then back to the other side of the counter, bracing his arms on the sides. "Lucy's maternal grandparents. Raina and Landon Dunkin. They think I'm unfit to raise Lucy. They say they're going to fight for custody."

She bolted up. "What? But anyone can see you're a great father. I can see that and I've been back in town for three days. Even the little things—the way you played thumb war with her at Hurley's tonight. Six times until your meals came. Letting her make a sundae out of her piece of cake."

He dropped down on one of the chairs and took a slug of his wine, gesturing for Annabel to come sit. "The Dunkins would say she shouldn't have had that piece of cake, that it's too much sugar. But then I let her add whipped cream too. God, maybe I *don't* think. Maybe I don't know how to do this, how to be a good father." His jaw was set hard, his expression grim as he leaned his head back and stared up at the ceiling.

She moved over with her own wine and sat down across from him. "Come on, a slice of cake? What could they really think is so terrible?"

"They came over earlier today when I burned my

attempt at French toast—the kitchen was all smoky, the smoke alarm blaring. And before that someone at the pediatrician's office tattled to them that Lucy was there today after falling out of a tree. She scraped up her leg pretty bad."

"I've had a few smoky kitchens in my day, and I'm a chef," she said. "It happens. And tree scrapes? That's childhood."

He seemed to calm down a bit, but then he stood up and started pacing again. "They think I'm unfit. And maybe they're right. Maybe I'm not the best dad. I know I'm not exactly a mother. But I love Lucy more than anything in the world. They can't take her from me."

Suddenly she understood why making scrambled eggs and chicken salad was worth a thousand bucks. He wanted to be a better father to prove to the Dunkins that he could take care of his daughter.

"Should I stop her from climbing trees? Should I make her wear dresses like Raina wants? Should I hire a housekeeper and cook even though the last one told Lucy she was a bad girl for leaving her action figures on the rug instead of putting them away? Another one forgot Lucy was allergic to soy and made her some supposedly healthy smoothie and Lucy ended up in the ER. I'm doing my best and it's not good enough. Never will be," he muttered, then stalked out of the kitchen.

She trailed after him. "Surely if you talk to them, explain how much you love her, that you're trying, that you're taking this intensive cooking class—"

"I called Raina before I brought Lucy over to the restaurant tonight. I told her I was really working at this, that you were teaching me to cook. 'Too little, too late, sorry,' was all she said before hanging up on me." He sat down on one of the red sofas, his head in his hands.

Annabel sat down beside him. She wanted to put her arm around him, assure him he'd get through this. Could the Dunkins really take his daughter away from him? The thought chilled her. She could just imagine what it did to West. "It's not too late for anything. You're a good father. You care. You're paying me a fortune to teach you to cook for your child. You love that girl and that's all that matters."

"It's not all that matters to the Dunkins. Apparently, if I really loved her, I wouldn't have done X, Y or Z." He turned and looked at her, his expression slowly changing from worry to determination. "But you're right, Annabel. It's not too late and I do care. So screw this useless moping. I'm not going to sit here and do nothing. I'm going to fight for my daughter. And one of those ways is to show them or the courts that I can take care of her. So let's continue with the lunch lesson."

And so they headed back into the kitchen, where Annabel taught him how to make chicken salad and baked chicken fingers, how to make a Cobb salad, how to make a perfect BLT. "Kids love chicken fingers," she said, sliding the tray of them in the oven. "You can keep these in the fridge and heat them up for Lucy tomorrow. At the last restaurant I worked at in Dallas, I offered children's cooking classes and the kids made these. I'll bet Lucy would love cooking with you."

"I saw how great you were with her at the restaurant," he said. "You'd be a great mother. I'm surprised you're not married with two kids already."

She stared at the floor, suddenly reminded that she'd better be careful of how much this man was getting inside her again. She made a show of looking at her watch. It was almost eleven-thirty. "I should get home," she said. "Maybe you could ask the Dunkins to stay for breakfast tomorrow morning when they drop off Lucy—you can show them your omelet skills."

"The smoky kitchen was the final straw. And they'll take her directly to school anyway. But thank you, Annabel," he said, holding her gaze. "I know I asked a lot of you and that I'm probably not your favorite person," he added.

She froze for a second. "That was a long time ago."

"Yeah."

A flash of memory came over her, of West kissing her so hard her knees buckled, of desire she'd never felt before or since rushing over every inch of her body. She took in West's warm brown eyes, the tangle of thick dark hair, the midnight stubble shadowing his square jaw. She tamped back the urge to reach a hand to his face. *Get back on track, Annabel. The right track*, she ordered herself. *Your thoughts are headed for a derailment.* She glanced down at her slip-on canvas sneakers to clear her mind of his face and body. Finally she looked back up. "You're a good father, West. Anyone can see that."

"Anyone but the Dunkins," he said. He walked her out to her car, the moonlight casting shadows on his face. "Thank you again, Annabel. For everything." He reached for her hand and squeezed it, a thank-you gesture, nothing more, but instead of letting go, he held on, his gaze moving from their entwined hands slowly up to her face, her lips, her eyes. He reached a hand to her cheek, and she leaned into his palm, her hand tightening on his.

And then he backed her slowly against the car, his mouth coming down on hers. She closed her eyes, reveling in the feel of his lips on hers. *West, West, West,* she thought.

"What am I doing?" he said suddenly, pulling away.

What was *she* doing? *Lord, Annabel.*

"I can't do this." He backed up, looking up at the sky, full of stars, distant lights of a plane inching across. "I'm sorry, Annabel. It just… I guess for a minute there I wanted to forget how insane my life is right now."

Red-hot anger—and a spiral of sadness—spun around her stomach. She was a placeholder—again. *Not.*

She turned around and opened her car door before she could slap him or unleash seven years' worth of *how dare you!* on him. His life *was* insane right now. It had been then. But that didn't mean he could…use her to forget that crazy life. No way, bucko. He wasn't attracted to her seven years ago; she wasn't his kind of girl, and she still wasn't.

She was about to let him have it, but when she turned around to face him, the look in his eyes—the worry, fear, torment—softened her ire and she found herself giving his hand a squeeze.

She looked up at the sky, trying to clear her mind. "I meant what I said, West. You're a good father and *you* should be raising Lucy. You. Just show them who you are."

"Maybe that's what I'm afraid of," he said so softly she wasn't sure she'd heard him right.

People always show you, tell you loud and clear, who they are, Gram's favorite saying running through her mind again. *It's up to you to be watching and listening, not ignoring red flags waving in the breeze because of a handsome face or smooth talk.*

Okay, so maybe West Montgomery wasn't a man to marry. The rebel in the leather jacket who broke your heart never was, right? But that didn't mean he was an unfit father. That she saw, heard with her own eyes and ears.

She squeezed his hand again and got in the car, tears stinging the backs of her eyes as she drove away, a glance in the rearview mirror letting her know he was still there, watching her go.

When West woke up in the morning, his stupidity punched him hard in the gut. Why the hell had he gone and kissed Annabel last night? Now he'd mucked things up with her, made things…weird. One minute, he'd been about to hold her car door open for her to say goodbye, and the next, what he saw in her eyes meant so much to him that he'd been overwhelmed and wanted to kiss her, wanted to soak up all that belief she had in him.

You're a good father, West. Anyone can see that.

Those two sentences had touched him so deeply, felt so good, that he wanted more. So he'd kissed her like a fool, when romance and women were off the table. And Annabel Hurley? That cut too deep. She was a reminder of how his parents had felt about him. She was a reminder of the kind of love he could have had if he hadn't let her go. She was a reminder that if *hadn't* dropped her for Lorna, there would be no Lucy. And she was a reminder that not one woman had ever stirred in him the kind of feelings she had and still did. He wanted to talk to Annabel, hear what she had to say and then pick her up in his arms and carry her to his bed.

And deep down, where things burned in his gut, his feelings for Annabel Hurley were just too…intense for him to deal with, which meant he had to shut them down. His focus had to be on Lucy, on keeping Lucy, on saving his family. Instead he was making out with Annabel Hurley in his front yard. "You're a bad father," he whispered, shame settling in his stomach. *So forget Annabel. Forget kissing her, forget what you want to do to her.*

The minute he tried to put Annabel and the kiss out of his head, he realized what else was burning in his gut—he had that same cold dread in his heart, snaking up his spine and wrapping around his nerve endings: Lucy wasn't here. Anytime she slept at the Dunkins', he was always aware of the lack of her. The world didn't seem right when she wasn't where she was supposed to be, which was here at—he glanced at the clock on his bedside table—5:30 a.m. She was on a regularly-scheduled sleepover at her grandparents and she'd be back home after school. But given what the Dunkins had threatened… Suddenly, West wanted his daughter here now, where she belonged. Home.

Normally he'd get out of bed, throw on his clothes and work boots and head out to the corrals and let the cattle out on the range. Then he'd come back, shower and dress and wake up his baby girl by pretend-cracking an egg over her head—that was her favorite way to wake up—and tickling his fingers down the sides of her face and under her chin to mimic the feel of gooey raw egg white and yolk. He'd give her a big hug and leave to let her get dressed.

So sometimes she'd come downstairs for breakfast in a pink church dress with red tights and her yellow light-up sneakers, and no, he wasn't going to tell her she didn't match. She matched fine. He'd try to untangle the knot at the side of her head, but sometimes he just couldn't get the darned thing loose. So off she'd go to school looking...unique.

This morning he had no doubt Raina had her wearing some scratchy school-appropriate outfit, her hair tangle free, her lunch box packed with healthful food.

West sat up and reached over to scratch Daisy, dozing as usual at the end of the bed, behind the ears. Maybe his daughter liked looking more presentable. Maybe she wore green and purple and crazy stripes because she didn't know better, not because she liked looking as if she'd dressed in a tornado. Lorna had made such a fuss over dressing Lucy just so, and Lucy had been stubborn, shaking her head and pointing at the outfit her mother wouldn't let her wear. Lorna had always won, of course; she'd been the parent, West realized, with the Dunkins' constant refrain: You're *the parent, West*, ringing in his ears.

He'd call Raina this morning, they'd talk it out, and she'd back down. He *was* the parent, damn it.

An hour later, his two ranch hands had arrived, and the three of them got the cattle out a bit father and the horses taken care of, then checked on the calves. Finally West showered and slurped down a strong cup of coffee, steeling himself for the call he had to make to Raina. He pressed in the numbers, his stomach clenching at the sound of Raina's hello. The call lasted all of forty seconds: *Lucy is just fine, and we're not changing our minds about seeking custody, sorry, but enough is enough, we just want our granddaughter raised right, goodbye, West.* Click.

That got West stewing for a bit until he hightailed it upstairs, put on his one suit and tie and got in his pickup, heading into town by 8:00 a.m to go see Winston Philips, a shark of a lawyer with a reputation for getting the job done. The man was known for working from 7:00 a.m. to be on par with eastern standard time until 7:00 p.m. He cost a mint, but so be it. If West had Winston Philips representing him, the Dunkins wouldn't be awarded custody of his daughter.

Except when West pulled into the parking lot, who was coming out of Philips's office but Raina and Landon Dunkin.

West cursed and let his head drop against the steering wheel, then drove over to the Blue Gulch elementary school and sat in his truck and looked for his daughter among the kids racing around the playground before the morning bell. He spotted Lucy and her friends Juliet and Delilah on the tire swing, and he wanted to go over and hug her so bad, but the bell rang and the kids shrieked and raced to line up.

At the front door of the school, he saw one of Lucy's little friends heading inside with her parents, each holding a hand and swinging her up. Her dad leaned down for a kiss and then she raced ahead, but her mom called her back, smiling and pointing at her Olaf lunch box still in her hand. The girl came running back, took her lunch box and then off she went.

At least five times over the past few months, West had gotten a call from the school office that Annabel had forgotten her lunch box and could he bring it down or should they bill him for a school lunch?

Lucy needs a mother, he thought numbly. Someone who could fix her knotty ringlets and remember to hand over her lunch box and notice if her pants were raggedy or the wrong color.

A mother.

West bolted upright, the lightbulb over his head so bright he had to blink. *Yes, that's it.*

Lucy did need a mother. And West needed a way to keep the Dunkins from taking Lucy from him.

Annabel Hurley was that way. The Dunkins liked Annabel. With Annabel as his wife, helping care for Lucy, they'd have no reason to sue for custody. Nor would they win as easily.

Annabel desperately needed money to save Hurley's. He desperately needed a wife to save his family. They could solve each other's problems and when things settled down, they could go their separate ways. A business deal from beginning to end, and together they'd work out the details of the middle.

He was due over to Hurley's tonight for the lesson on appetizers. Somewhere, between rolling biscuit batter around little hot dogs, he'd ask her to marry him.

He'd imagined that once before, a fleeting thought in the barn loft seven years ago, when he'd felt things he'd never felt before and never had with Lorna, even when he'd started to actually care for his reckless wife. But now it had nothing to do with feelings and everything to do with making sure the most important things in their lives weren't wrenched away.

He had no idea if Annabel would go for it. But he'd vowed to do anything he could to save his family and *he* was going for it.

In fact, forget about waiting for class tonight. There was no time to waste. It was a three-minute walk from where he was parked now to Hurley's Homestyle Kitchen.

Which meant he had three minutes to figure out exactly how he was going to propose a business deal of a marriage to a woman who might not even be speaking to him anymore.

Chapter Four

In the restaurant kitchen, Annabel was mashing potatoes for garlic smashed potatoes—every smash a
reminder to squash her feelings for West. Across the island, Hattie added onions and homemade bread crumbs
to a big bowl of ground beef for meat loaf. Five loaves
were already in the oven for the lunch rush, which began
at eleven in a ranch town, and the smell, even at eight-
thirty in the morning, was delectable. Annabel had
grown up on cold meat loaf sandwiches in her brown-
bagged lunch, packed by her mother and then her gram,
and it would always be her favorite comfort food.

Hattie glanced out the window and upped her chin.
"Looks like someone's moving into the old take-out
place."

Annabel squinted against the morning sunshine and
looked across the street to the formerly empty store-

front between the Blue Gulch Bakery and Yoga For You. "Coming Soon! Clyde's Burgertopia!" she read.

Annabel's stomach dropped. Everyone knew Clyde Heff made amazing burgers on his grill at his exclusive annual backyard Fourth of July parties. The key was apparently some kind of "secret ingredient" dating back five generations, and Annabel was pretty sure the secret ingredient was a mixture of bourbon and dill. But the man could make a mean burger, and now he'd be pulling lunch and dinner customers away from Hurley's. Granted, that little storefront with the small back room couldn't handle more than a counter and takeout business. But still. It was competition. Competition Hurley's didn't need. Worse, Clyde's daughter, Francie, had been part of Lorna Dunkin's posse back in middle school and high school.

Laughter, then: *Oh my God, Geekabel, those suede flats are like from the '80s. Get a clue.* Those suede flats had been her mother's, and Annabel cherished them. Or she'd find herself behind Lorna and Francie and their friends on the lunch line at school and hear, *I'd kill to be as skinny as Geekabel but only if I could keep my 32-Cs and my tiny waist. I mean, what's the point of being a rail if you look like a boy?* Then laughter, firm agreement and discussion. Annabel couldn't imagine snooty Francie Heff eating something as common as a burger, even at her father's own restaurant, so maybe she wouldn't have to see much of her old tormentor. If she did, Annabel would just stare her down and give it right back to her.

Eyeing the sign announcing the Burgertopia again, Annabel thought of the bills and the amount left in Gram's business account. Plus, a quarterly loan payment was coming due soon. Her stomach churned and panic crawled up her spine. "Between Sau Lin's noodle shop, the new steak house and the Burgertopia, we'll have a trickle of customers. I'm all for new businesses opening in town, but we're in trouble."

If only there were money to build the back patio the way Gram had always dreamed, surrounded by the beautiful oaks and the wildflowers. They could put a children's playground back there and hire a sitter so people could eat dinner in peace. They could break down the wall to the too-big hallway and add five tables to the main dining room. They could spruce up the place with warm yellow paint and new dishware and cutlery. They could hire a full-time cook to take the pressure off her and Hattie, someone as great as Essie's former longtime assistant cook, Martha, who knew the recipes inside and out but had long ago moved to Austin.

These were all ideas that couldn't come to fruition. There was barely money to pay the bills. And with the loan coming due in a month and very little hope to pay it...

Hattie covered Annabel's hand and patted it. "Listen, all we can do is make the best food we know how and keep folks coming in." She added Worcestershire sauce to the meat loaf, Annabel comforted by the fact that Gram's century-old recipe, handed down from her mother, was the best meat loaf anyone had ever had.

Yes. Focus on making the best chicken-fried steak and meat loaf and braised short ribs and garlic mashed potatoes and po'boy sandwiches—like the ones that West loved so much—in the county, she told herself. That was what Gram had always said. *Just focus on being the best you you can be and don't worry about anyone else.*

Why did she have to bring West into the equation? A man who kissed and took it back. A man who broke her heart so irrevocably she felt split in two for over a year. A man who'd hurt her so badly she'd been dumb enough to let her heartbreak control her, keeping her away from home, from her gram, from Clem, for so long.

She'd never let that happen again. She might still believe in love, but she'd never be a dummy about it again—that was for sure. Though she wondered if a person could help it, if you were swept away and caught up and couldn't control it. There were people like her friend Sally from Dallas who specifically looked for a husband she liked who met her long list of criteria, including big salary and lack of family history of cancer and male pattern baldness. Annabel had gone to her wedding, and Sally had looked awfully happy with her wealthy husband with his head full of thick hair, a man Sally liked and admired but didn't love. Then there was Annabel's cousin Susannah clear across Texas who'd fallen madly in love with a hilarious, kind bull rider with no money, married him in a whirlwind wedding three weeks later and was madly in love ten years later, with two little cowboys and three dogs.

Annabel let out a deep sigh. She had no idea how love worked or was supposed to work.

Ugh, what was she doing? She had to focus on saving Hurley's Homestyle Kitchen, not worry about her love life or lack thereof. When it came to West Montgomery, she had to protect her heart and keep her lips at a distance. Two feet away at all times. That way, if he tried to kiss her again, he'd fall over and land flat on his face, as it should be.

"Now, that's a much better sight than a new sign going up across the street," Hattie said, winking at Annabel.

Huh? Annabel glanced out the window and there was the man himself crossing the street, looking very... serious. West, in a suit and tie, strangely enough, was about to pass through the open gate leading to the restaurant, but then he turned tail, jogging back across the street, paced from the yoga studio down to the Blue Gulch Public Library and back again. He stood there, across the street, hands on hips, as though he was working something out with himself.

Good Lord, was he about to come in here and tell her he wanted his money back for the lessons, prorated for the breakfast and lunch ones he'd had, that he'd hire someone else?

Or maybe something had progressed with the Dunkins in their threat to try to get custody of Lucy. Maybe that was what the suit and tie was about. Had he already been to court his morning?

"Interesting," Hattie said, eyebrow raised as West paced down to the library again, then back, crossing the street with a look of pure determination in his face, as though whatever was yanking him around inside his brain wouldn't win out. He stood by the window and glanced in and when he spotted Annabel, he held up a hand, then jogged up the steps.

Annabel shrugged at Hattie, wiped her hands on her apron and went out the front door to the porch.

"Do you have a few minutes?" he asked. "Maybe more than a few minutes. I need to talk to you."

"Let me just tell Hattie to cover my potatoes." In moments she was back, apron off.

They walked down Blue Gulch Street toward the town green with its pretty wood gazebo and American flag. He stopped in front of a stone bench, and gestured for her to sit down, then sat beside her, loosening his blue-and-red-striped tie.

"I'm in this getup—" he gestured at his suit jacket "—because I'd planned to go see Winston Philips this morning, to hire him as my attorney to fight the Dunkins. But when I pulled into the lot, the Dunkins were coming out of his office. They mean business, Annabel." He cleared his throat. "And so do I. So I have a proposition for you."

She stared at him. "A proposition?" What proposition? Just then, a couple walking their little dachshund strolled by, so she had to wait until they said their hellos and asked West how his daughter was and if he had any ponies for sale, which he did, and get through five more minutes of them setting up a date and time to come out to the ranch. Finally they waved and walked away, the little dog stopping to sniff something, and Annabel wanted to scream at the top of her lungs, *Move along already, people!*

West took her hand and led her over to the narrow cobblestone alley between the park and Blue Gulch Coffee and Treats. "Just so there are no more interruptions." He glanced down, then up at her. "You've said Hurley's is in big financial trouble. I'm willing to take care of the bills, payroll, the loan in its entirety and flesh out the business account with enough capital for improvements. I'll make sure Hurley's stays open and give you the breathing room so that the restaurant can start turning a profit again."

She stared at him, joy fluttering for a moment as she heard only that Hurley's Homestyle Kitchen would be saved. Then her fairy godfather morphed back into West when she recalled the word *proposition*, which meant he wanted something from her.

"And in return, I…?"

"You marry me."

Annabel's jaw dropped. *"What?"*

He shoved his hands in his pockets. "I need a wife—a wife the Dunkins will approve of—to keep them from fighting me for custody. They like you, they like your family. You're a chef, you always look nice, you'll know how to take care of Lucy in a way that will satisfy them. I'm desperate here, Annabel. I need you to marry me—for however long it takes to show them I'm a good father, for me to learn from you how to be more of a mother too. If in six months or a year, whenever, we're all good, then we can quietly go our separate ways. I know it's a lot to ask, but I'm offering a lot in return."

Annabel leaned back against the brick wall of the coffee shop, needing something to brace herself against. Good God. West wanted her to marry him—a sham marriage—to keep his daughter. This was serious stuff. The man she'd always loved, still loved, damn it, was proposing marriage. For the sake of his family. It was both awful and understandable at the same time.

It *was* a lot to ask. And he *was* offering a lot in return.

"I need to go, West," she said, feeling those stupid tears stinging her eyes again. "I need to process this, okay?"

He put his hands on her shoulders, and she looked up at him. "I wouldn't ask this of you if I didn't have to."

Yeah, West, I know *that. Jerk!*

It was just like him to make it worse.

"I need to think," she said again, and took off running.

Lunchtime was so busy at Hurley's that Annabel barely had time to think about West's proposition. But she'd been so distracted that she'd forgotten that table six had asked for coleslaw with the meat loaf and not the garlic mashed potatoes, forgot about table ten's order entirely, then attempted to plate the fried green tomatoes and instead dropped them on the floor and stepped on one, which squished under her clog.

"You all right?" Clementine asked, searching her face. "I've never seen you so disorganized." She put a bunch of orders on her tray and added the sour pickle to table five's roast beef po'boy. Annabel had forgotten the pickle.

"I'm fine," Annabel said, running the back of her hand across her forehead. "Just got something on my mind."

Clementine eyed her again, made up a few baskets of fried mushrooms, and put those on her tray. "I'll keep the hordes satisfied with these till you can get those orders up. I'll have Harold come in and help."

"That's a good idea," Annabel said, hating to let everyone down by messing up. This was her world—she'd grown up in this kitchen, had shucked corn and rinsed vegetables and knew how to spell every spice by the time she was six—and she'd spent seven years in upscale Dallas restaurants. She knew better than to allow distractions to get in the way of work.

Harold arrived ten minutes later. They all got into a groove, the food served and happy customers leaving nice tips.

Finally, the dining room empty, the kitchen cleaned and dinner prepped, Annabel prepared a lunch tray for her grandmother and headed down the hall to Essie's bedroom. How she wished she could tell her gram about West's proposal, but her grandmother was frail enough without worrying that Annabel would marry a man who didn't love her to save the family business. Gram would tell her not to marry West, so Annabel decided to keep the proposal to herself for the time being.

Her grandmother's room faced the backyard with her beloved vegetable garden where they grew most of the produce and herbs they needed for the restaurant. Annabel knocked and at Gram's "Come on in," she carried in the tray of soup and sweet tea.

"Great news, Gram," Annabel said, setting down the tray on the swing-out table at Essie's bedside. "Lunch was very busy today. Not a lull and a line out on the porch. The potato leek chowder and fried catfish po'boy with Creole mayonnaise were big hits."

"I can see why," Gram said, tasting the chowder. "No one makes soup like you, Annabel."

Annabel smiled at her grandmother, her silvery white hair in a neat bun—Clementine's doing. "You taught me."

Essie Hurley put down her spoon and stared down, her expression falling. "I'm glad to hear business was good today, sweetheart, but I've been meaning to tell you... I—" She glanced away, then back. "The restau-

rant is in bigger trouble than I let on. I don't know if
you've had a chance to look through the books. I was
hoping Georgia would come home and maybe see if
anything could be done at this point, but between the
competition and my health failing, it looks like Hurley's Homestyle Kitchen might have to close its doors.
And that's okay, sweetie. You've got a life in Dallas,
and maybe if I close up shop, Clementine will have a
chance to see the great big world out there instead of
spending her life waitressing at her family restaurant."

Annabel saw the resignation in her grandmother's
face, the pain in her eyes. Essie Hurley had started Hurley's fifty years ago as a twenty-five-year-old newlywed,
been through ups and downs, including the loss of her
beloved husband and then her only son and daughter-
in-law. If Annabel could help it, she wouldn't let her
grandmother, especially in her condition, suffer the loss
of her beloved restaurant.

"Gram, first of all, Clementine is exactly where she
wants to be. She's a small-town girl and loves Blue
Gulch. And second, I have no interest in going back to
Dallas. I want to be here with you and Clem and work in
the kitchen. And third, there's no way we'll let Hurley's
close. We'll get through this, just as you always have.
And if today's any indication, business is picking up."

Annabel wasn't sure what to say about Georgia not
coming home. Where her older sister was—why she
wasn't coming when she was needed—that was just
as worrisome as the possibility of losing Hurley's. But
Georgia had to have a damned good reason for staying away.

Tears pooled in Gram's blue eyes. "We've had good
days in the past too. I'm a fact facer and numbers don't

lie. I've had a good run, Annabel. Fifty wonderful years. It'll be okay, honey."

Tears pricked Annabel's eyes too, a combination of anger and determination keeping them at bay. She could plainly see it wouldn't be okay. And losing Hurley's might be just the thing to push her frail grandmother over the edge. "Gram, listen to me. I'm not letting Hurley's close. I'll make some kind of deal with the bank. I'll do what I have to do. But Hurley's will not close."

Her grandmother slipped her hand into hers. There was no way she'd let her gram down. Essie Hurley had taken in her three granddaughters when their parents died, putting aside her own grief over losing her son to be there for three young teenagers who'd howled in pain every night and walked around like zombies during the day for weeks until the shock had settled some. Annabel would not let the bank take away the one thing that had sustained her grandmother, sustained their family, all these years.

I'm willing to take care of the bills, payroll, the loan in its entirety and flesh out the business account with enough capital for improvements. I'll make sure Hurley's stays open and give you the breathing room so that the restaurant can start turning a profit again.

She needed West.

He needed her.

To be honest, he'd had her at "marry me to save my daughter." If a sham marriage would save his family, she'd have married him for that reason alone. That he could save Hurley's would just make it all easier to swallow.

Essie's eyes drifted closed, so Annabel quietly picked up the lunch tray and carried it back to the kitchen. She pulled out her phone and texted West: I'll see you at 9:15 at your house for the appetizer lesson.

She'd get through the dinner rush at the restaurant without dropping a plate of fried green tomatoes or confusing the sides. On her breaks, she'd work up her list of questions—and, boy, did she have questions—about how exactly this "marriage" would be set up. You could fool a lot of people, but you couldn't fool a kid—nor would Annabel want to, and she was sure West wasn't willing to do anything that would confuse Lucy.

Immediately three more questions popped into her head, one that made her blush. She should really write these down.

Is that a no to my proposal? West texted back.

You still need to know how to make bruschetta & healthy snacks for Lucy, she texted. Wife or no wife.

She quickly added: PS—I have questions about how this is gonna work.

Me too, he texted back. And now I'm hopeful you might say yes.

God help me, she thought.

How is *this going to work?* West wondered as he peeked in on Lucy, fast asleep in her bedroom. He tiptoed in and moved a ringlet of hair off her face, and she shifted, squeezing the stuffed Eeyore her mother had given her for Christmas a few years ago. He moved the pink and white blanket up to just under her chin, his heart constricting.

"I'll do anything for you," he whispered to his daughter, touching a kiss to her forehead before slipping back out of her room.

As he headed into the kitchen to brew a pot of coffee—

he had a feeling he and Annabel would need the strong stuff—he tried to think about how the business marriage would be set up. They'd have to look like a real couple, of course, share a home, a bedroom.

A bedroom.

His phone vibrated in his pocket. A text from Annabel to say she was here, on the porch.

He opened the door, and there she stood, carrying a grocery bag. Her long, silky auburn hair was loose around her shoulders, and though she had on a long, thick, open cardigan, the white T-shirt she wore, tucked into tight jeans, her feet in flip-flops, her toenails painted a shimmery red, made him want to grab her close and just hug her, to breathe in the scent of her. What he felt was something like…need, and it unnerved him. He stepped back and held the door open wide.

She offered a tight smile. "I didn't want to risk waking Lucy by ringing the doorbell."

"That's exactly one of the reasons why you're perfect to play this part," he said, taking the grocery bag. "You think of things like that and you're not even a parent."

A strained look crossed her face, but then it disappeared and she started for the kitchen. He followed her in. "I brought lots of fruit and vegetables." She pulled produce out of the bag onto the island. She slid over an almost empty bowl that had once been full of fruit and stacked apples and oranges and a bunch of bananas inside. "After school, when Annabel gets home, she can just grab an apple, and you can show her how to spread a little peanut butter on slices for added protein, and—"

"Annabel," he interrupted, taking both her hands and stilling them. She was talking a mile a minute, and he'd bet his truck she was nervous as hell about what they really needed to talk about—and Lucy's after-school snack wasn't it.

"So I guess I'd move in," she said, glancing everywhere but at him. She finally looked up at him.

He nodded and let go of her hands. "For all intents and purposes, as they say, it will be a real marriage. For as long as necessary," he added quickly, wanting to make sure she knew there was an out, that she wouldn't be stuck with him forever. "Why don't we have some coffee and sit down and talk it out?"

She nodded, wrapping her cardigan sweater around herself and sitting at the kitchen table, the low sliver of moon just visible in the bay window. He handed her a mug of coffee and watched her slowly add cream and a spoonful of sugar. It was clear she needed a minute before he launched into the mechanics of their would-be marriage.

"A real marriage," she repeated. "I'm confused by that because...because a real marriage is based on a few things that aren't going on between the two of us." She wagged her finger back and forth from him to her.

He sat down and took a sip of his coffee. "Well, I guess I mean a real marriage in the sense that we'll live in the same house, share a bedroom, act like husband and wife when we're in public."

"Share a bedroom," she said slowly. "For appearances' sake, you mean."

He held her gaze, and as her cheeks slightly pinkened he was consumed by the urge to rush over to her and kiss her, to take off that thick beige sweater and slowly undress her, feel her hair slide down his chest, let his hands roam where they wanted. She looked away and wrapped her own hands around the coffee mug.

He'd gone back and forth on this one. He thought that keeping things "professional" in their business marriage was the smartest thing to do; after all, this whole marriage would be about Lucy, about him being a better father, about him able to be a father. It wasn't about sex. But then he started thinking of the effect Annabel had on him and the reality of sleeping next to her every night. Maybe they could fulfill certain needs while still keeping things…businesslike.

Daisy ambled over to sniff Annabel's foot, which gave him a few seconds before he had answer. A wrong word and she might sprint out the door.

"Not necessarily, no," he said. "I mean, we'll be sharing a bedroom. Every night. Sleeping in the same bed, inches apart. But if you want to keep things strictly platonic, I'll abide by that. I'm just saying that I'm a man and you're a woman and you'll be an inch away from me in bed." The memory of her, half-dressed underneath him in the hayloft of his family's barn, came slowly into his mind, the feel of her lips, how soft her skin was, how badly he'd wanted her.

She nodded slowly, and he was dying to know what she was thinking. Had he offended her? Was it too much to want sex on top of everything else he was asking? She had to know the effect she had on him, had always had on him. How was he supposed to resist her? He would, of course, if that was what she wanted.

"Let's leave that one for later discussion," she said, giving Daisy a rub under her chin. The dog jumped on the window seat and curled up, snoozing in seconds flat. "What about Lucy? What are you going to tell her?"

He took a long slug of his coffee. "I'm going to tell her that the nice lady who helped her make a cake sundae at Hurley's the other day is a wonderful person and that I've decided to marry her. Seems like enough information for a six-year-old."

Annabel nodded. "And the Dunkins? Is that what you're going to tell them?"

A chill ran up his spine. "I'll tell the Dunkins that I've decided it would be in my and Lucy's best interests if I had a good wife who'd make a wonderful mother."

"Aren't they going to ask if you love this good wife who'd make a wonderful mother?"

"They don't care if I love you. They care that you'll be a proper influence on Lucy and make sure she's taken care of."

Again, Annabel nodded. "And so I'll make healthful family meals, keep Lucy's ringlets tangle free, make sure she's dressed in a way that doesn't set Raina Dunkin flying into the attorney's office, catch her if she falls from that crab apple tree and then in a few months or so we'll reevaluate the need for the marriage?" For a moment her dark brown eyes looked so sad that he froze, but she sipped her coffee and her expression changed, back to business.

"That's it exactly," he said, relieved that she so completely understood what was necessary. *What was necessary.* The whole thing stank—even if she did agree to sex. West didn't like having his hands tied, being forced into something, especially something as sacred as marriage and vows.

He stood up and paced the length of the kitchen, mad as hell suddenly that he was being forced—and that he was asking something like this of Annabel. He was tying her hands too—how could she *not* help him? And how could she not after he was dangling his bank account in front of her when her family business was in jeopardy?

Sometimes he really did feel every bit the jerk his parents, the Dunkins and a few women in town thought him to be. He guessed he should include Annabel in that group too.

Hell.

He tried to imagine how his parents would react if they were alive to hear the news that he was marrying Annabel Hurley. His father would probably tell him he was proud of him for the first time. His mother would worry for Annabel's heart, mind and soul. He'd loved his parents and he hated thinking of them this way, but yeah, it burned to know he'd finally win their approval with a sham marriage. It just figured. What was real didn't matter. Everything was about appearances. It had always been that way with his parents. And it was that way with the Dunkins.

And then there was Annabel. A woman who probably wished she'd never had to lay eyes on him again after what he did to her seven years ago. Now he'd talked her into marrying him to save her family's business.

He suddenly felt sick to his stomach, red-hot anger churning in his gut. "You know what, Annabel, I think we're done here. Peanut butter on apple slices. A banana. I got it. You're clear on the marriage arrangement. So let's call it a night."

She stared at him for a moment. "Well, if *you're* all set."

Sarcasm. He sighed, wishing he could explain everything bashing around in his head. "Do you have more questions? Something we didn't cover?" The weariness in his voice surprised even him and he sat back down.

She seemed to be considering something but then got up and wrapped the sweater tightly around herself again. "We're crystal clear," she said, reaching over to give Daisy a scratch on her head before heading toward the door.

"Anything we didn't agree on tonight or talk about we'll just deal with as it comes up," he said, thinking about Annabel lying next to him in bed, naked and beautiful. Though she likely wouldn't be naked. Damn it. He'd have to keep his hands to himself. It was bad enough he was putting her in this position. He wasn't going to come on to her and complicate things with sex, no matter how much he wanted her. That was what cold showers and mucking out stalls were for. There. He'd made the decision for them. No sex. Platonic. Businesslike.

"I assume you want to get married as soon as possible," she said, walking into the living room.

He followed her. "This Friday at the town hall?"

She stopped and turned to face him. Again, something crossed her features that he wasn't sure of. Like a Friday afternoon wedding at the Blue Gulch town hall was any woman's idea of a dream wedding, even for a sham marriage. *Good God, West.*

"That's just fine," she said, an edge in her voice. "I'll have Harold cover for me. I might even be able to work the dinner shift."

West might not know Annabel all that well yet, but he knew sarcasm when he heard it.

She burst into tears, covering her face with her hands.

He stepped close and moved her hands away, tilting

up her chin. He hated to see her cry, see such a kind person in such turmoil. Because of him. "Hey. I'm sorry, Annabel. I'm sorry I'm asking this of you. I'm sorry."

She sucked in a breath and wiped at her eyes. "You're going to save Hurley's. I'm going to help keep your family together. It's worth it."

"Yeah." He nodded. It was worth it. For both of them. "We'll make it work for ourselves, whatever that means, okay?"

She bit her lip and let out another breath. "Okay. Now that I'm thinking about it, I'm not sure we'll have all the ducks in a row for the town hall Friday, West. We should probably just fly to Las Vegas. That way, nosy eyes and ears at the town hall won't be gossiping about us and the ceremony all over town."

"Vegas," he repeated, thinking a trip to the Strip with its fun and lights would be much more special than the Blue Gulch Town Hall. But then again, there was the matter of the wedding night, and a hotel overnight in Vegas would mean...options. So maybe that wasn't such a great idea. Hadn't he just decided keeping his hands off her was the right thing?

But...they'd have a chance to be alone for their first night as a married couple and could figure out how they were going to handle sharing a bedroom. "Yeah. Much better idea anyway. I'll make the arrangements."

Then she was out the door so fast he couldn't even walk her to her car, watching the red taillights as she sent dust flying behind her.

Chapter Five

In the morning, Annabel and Clementine had their breakfast in Gram's room as they always did. As Annabel sat on a chair near the window, pushing scrambled eggs around on her plate, she wondered for the millionth time if she should just tell them the truth. The whole truth. But she couldn't; that wouldn't be fair to West. He needed everyone to believe this was a real marriage.

Then again, she wouldn't be lying if her family asked her if she loved West. Heck yeah, she loved him. He just didn't love her. Annabel tried to focus on Clementine filling in Gram on all the action in the dining room last night—Seth Barlow had proposed to his girlfriend of two weeks, and she'd told him they should wait at least a month; the Otterman twins, Marley and Michelle, came in as they did every week and ordered the same dish, the blackened chicken po'boy, with the same sides, sweet potato fries and coleslaw; June Davino got a standing ovation when she loudly told her husband that yes, she *did* think she should order the chocolate custard pie, and didn't need anyone being her food police.

That last one got a chuckle out of Gram. "Good for her!" Gram sipped her herbal tea, which she didn't like, but the doc had said no caffeine. "You've been quiet, Annabel. Everything all right?"

Annabel looked up and smiled at her grandmother. There was her in. *Just come out with it, Annabel.* "Well, actually..." she began, poking at her eggs with her fork. "I have news. Big news."

Gram sat up a bit and Clementine put down her coffee cup.

Annabel sucked in a deep breath. *Here goes everything*, she thought. "West Montgomery proposed and I accepted." She said it so fast she wondered if they'd caught it.

"Proposed what?" Clementine asked, picking up a piece of bacon.

"Marriage," Annabel said, realizing she should have added that bit. She and West had been reunited for what, a few days? And now they were getting hitched? Of course it would sound crazy.

The bacon halted in midair. "Wait. You and West Montgomery are getting married?" Clementine said. "Did I miss the relationship?" She looked all around the room, a teasing glint in her eyes.

"Well, you know I've been giving him cooking lessons," Annabel said, looking from her sister to her grandmother, "and things just kind of took off. He proposed."

Gram reached for Annabel's hand and clasped it between hers. "I know how much you loved West all those years ago. I suppose you two picked up where you left off seven years ago, finally together as you should be. I'm very happy for you, honey."

Oh, Gram, Annabel thought, her heart pinging.

"Me too," Clementine said, putting the bacon down and coming over for a hug. "Have you picked a date? June bride and all that? I'm sure you can find a beautiful gown by then, and of course, I'll take care of the all the arrangements. Ooh, I should call—"

"We've decided to elope to Las Vegas on Friday," Annabel said quickly. "We both want our marriage to start right away, so no fussy wedding. We just want to start our lives together." That was true, at least.

Annabel caught Gram and Clementine glancing at each other, their eyebrows raised, but the sweetness in their expressions told Annabel that despite knowing something was up, they were happy for her. They did both know how deep her feelings for West ran, and they knew she was a smart, sensible person. If she'd said yes, she knew what she was doing. Thank God for family who understood you—questioned you when you needed to be, challenged you when you needed to be, stayed quiet when they should because they understood you.

They didn't even bat an eyelash when she mentioned they should keep the news to themselves until she and West left on Friday, to give West a chance to tell his daughter and the Dunkins, if he hadn't already.

Gram trained her shrewd blue eyes on Annabel. "You tell that handsome fiancé of yours to stop by before you leave for Las Vegas. I want to give him my blessing."

Annabel nodded. The elderly woman might not be in the best health, but that determined look in her eye told Annabel that West was going to have to earn that blessing.

* * *

On Thursday night, West tried the French toast recipe
again, with a side of Lucy's favorite sausage and cut-up
fruit. No smoke alarm went off. Success. The French
toast was just plain edible, not like the batch he'd made
under Annabel's tutelage, but better than barely edible,
which was his usual grade.

As Lucy poured a little maple syrup on her plate,
West decided it was now or never.

"Sweets, remember that nice woman who invited
you into the kitchen at Hurley's to make your own slice
of cake sundae?"

Lucy nodded and put down the syrup. "Annabel Hurley. I saw her yesterday when Nana and I were passing
the restaurant. She waved at me. Nana waved at her too."

Well, that was good. "I've decided to marry Annabel."

Lucy gasped, joy lighting her face. "I'm going to
have a stepmother?"

West nodded. "What do you think of that?"

Lucy clapped the way she did when she was excited,
but then her expression turned somber. "Maddy Higgins
got a new stepmother because her mother died too," she
said, looking down at her lap. "I miss Mommy."

"Your mama will always be your mommy in here,"
West said, touching his heart and coming around the
table to scoop Lucy up in his arms. He patted her heart.
"Right in there. Always."

Lucy titled her head, her hazel eyes curious. "What
do stepmothers do?"

"Well, Annabel will make you much better breakfasts and dinners than I do. And she'll pack you amazing lunches. She'll help comb out your hair after your
baths. She'll help you get dressed, help you with your

homework, teach you to do cartwheels, play hide-and-seek, sing you lullabies at bedtime, hug you if you're feeling sad about anything."

"That sounds really good, Daddy. When will she be my stepmother?"

Relief washed over him. "We're getting married tomorrow," he said, gently twisting one of her dark ringlets around his finger. "And we'll be back the day after, on Saturday, I'm not sure what time yet. So definitely starting Sunday when you wake up, Annabel will be your stepmother."

"I'm really happy I'm getting a stepmother and that it's Annabel Hurley," she said. "She's so nice."

West held his daughter tightly, relieved at how the conversation went. "I'm going to tell your grandparents tomorrow morning. I think they'll be happy you'll have Annabel to help take good care of you."

He was 99.9 percent sure they'd not only back off from the custody threat, but back off, period. No matter how crazy things got, how strange it felt to marry a woman in a business arrangement, a marriage that was meant to be temporary, he had to remember the whole point was Lucy. Keeping his baby girl, his heart, his life.

Later that night, Lucy tucked in, his own version of a lullaby helping her drift off to sleep in record time, West went outside and stared up at the stars, hoping like hell this would all work out. He said a quick prayer for his brother, then for his parents, and as he was about to call Daisy over to head back into the house, he latched onto another star and said a prayer for himself.

Friday morning at ten, with assurances that Hattie and Harold could handle lunch and dinner, Annabel

waited on the porch for West to pick her up. The plan
was to fly to Las Vegas, stay over—for appearances—
then return Saturday late afternoon. Annabel figured
that way West wouldn't be more than a night away from
his daughter and Annabel could return to work at the
restaurant, which sorely needed her.

Clutching her overnight bag too tightly, Annabel told
herself to breathe, to calm down. But when the silver
pickup pulled up and turned into Hurley's tiny lot, Annabel's stomach flipped over and her ears felt as if they
were stuffed with cotton.

West jogged up the three steps. "All set?"

"My grandmother would like to give you her blessing," Annabel told him. "I'm not entirely sure what that
will entail—just warning you."

"Gotcha," he said, and followed her into the house.

"So, did you have any big conversations today?" Annabel asked on the way to Essie's room.

He nodded. "I told Lucy over dinner last night that
the pretty woman who helped her make her sundae cake
was going to be her stepmother and live with us at the
ranch. She's happy about it."

Annabel blew out a sigh of relief. "What about the
Dunkins?"

West leaned against the wall across from Essie's
room. "I called them this morning. Raina must have
said, 'Well, this certainly does change things,' at least
three times. They both sang your praises, how you come
from such a lovely family, that a woman with your background would certainly make an appropriate stepmother
for Lucy. Oh—and the Dunkins expect us for dinner
on Sunday."

Annabel's eyes widened. "Well, we'll just get through it, won't we?"

West nodded. "That's the name of the game."

At the reminder that they *were* playing something of a game, Annabel felt the wind knocked out of her a bit. She needed a minute to herself, so she knocked on her grandmother's door. "Gram? West has come to talk before we leave for the airport." Annabel had already said her goodbyes to her gram fifteen minutes ago and had Essie's beautiful antique wedding dress and veil in a garment bag. At first, she hadn't been sure she should wear such a symbol of true love to her own sham wedding, but her grandmother had said it would mean the world to her that Annabel wear her gown, so of course she would.

"Oh, good, send him in, dear," Gram said now.

West headed in, shutting the door behind him.

Annabel bit her lip and paced the hall, then figured she'd better go say goodbye to Clementine while she was alone. She found her sister setting up the dining room for lunch, Clem's long brown hair in a high ponytail.

"Next time you see me, I'll be a married woman," Annabel said.

Clementine whirled around. "Listen to me, Annabel Hurley. I know something's up. I don't know what, but I know you and I know you wouldn't be marrying West unless you loved him, no matter what else. So even though my 'say what?' alarm is a tiny bit raised, I'm very happy for you."

Annabel smiled. "I do love him, Clem. So much and so deep down in my blood and bones that I'm afraid of it."

"I know that feeling," Clementine said softly, her blue eyes clouding over for a moment.

Wait, she did? "Clem—"

"Ready?" West called from the doorway. "Oh, hi, Clementine," he added.

Clementine walked Annabel to the door, gave West a hug and her congratulations, then stepped out with them onto the porch.

"West, why don't you put my bags in the car while I say goodbye to my sister?"

He smiled and grabbed her two bags and headed across the street.

"I shouldn't have said anything," Clementine said. "I'm fine. But yes, I know the feeling all too well."

"I'm both happy and sad that you know. Love can be both the greatest and the worst feeling, huh?" She was dying to know who Clementine was talking about, who'd managed to win her guarded sister's heart.

"Exactly." Clem glanced across the street where West was waiting. "You'd better go. Can't be late for your own wedding."

Annabel hugged her sister again, then hurried to the car. West opened her door for her, waited until she was buckled, then got in the driver's side.

Annabel glanced across the street at the faded apricot Victorian, the beautiful old house she'd grown up in as a teenager, the half-century-old restaurant where she'd learned to cook at her grandmother's hip. Everything that needed to be okay—Hurley's, West's ability to keep his daughter—would be okay in just a few hours, with an *I do* and a kiss.

She heard West turning the key in the ignition and

snapped back to attention. "So, what did my grand-mother say?"

"She said if I hurt you, I'd answer to her."

Annabel smiled. But there was very little doubt that West would hurt her. Hurley's would be saved, West's family would be saved. But Annabel's heart would even-tually be irrevocably broken.

Chapter Six

True to his word, West had made all the arrangements. He'd booked a hotel room—one room, he'd told Annabel, so they'd have a chance to get used to "living together," prepaid for a four-fifteen time slot at an elegant chapel without a theme or a costumed officiant, and after a quick trip to the marriage bureau for their license, they had almost an hour to get ready.

Annabel looked around the fancy hotel room—West had spared no expense—her gaze stopping on the closed bathroom door. West had disappeared inside with his garment bag, containing his one suit, she assumed—and for that she was grateful. Getting used to living together by sharing a bedroom was one thing. Watching him take off his traveling clothes, seeing West even just half-naked, and getting dressed for their wedding was another.

She couldn't stop staring at the king-size bed in the middle of it all.

Tonight, when it was time to lie down in that bed, she'd be Mrs. Annabel Hurley Montgomery. How many times had she doodled that on her notebook paper while doing her homework in middle school and high school? Thousands of times.

"It's fine with you if I keep my last name as my middle name?" Annabel called through the bathroom door from where she stood staring out the window at the Las Vegas Strip, at the throngs of people walking, the lit-up fancy hotels and fountains and glamour. "I figure the Dunkins will expect me to be Annabel Montgomery. But I don't have a middle name, so I like the idea of keeping Hurley."

"Of course," he called back. "Annabel Hurley Montgomery, it is. It's probably better for business too."

Business. Right. It was good that one of them was constantly reminding her what this marriage was about.

When he came out, he wore a tuxedo and shiny black shoes, and he looked so damned handsome she gasped. "I clean up well, don't I?"

She couldn't take her eyes off him. "You sure do."

He laughed. "Your turn. Unless you want to get married in a tank top and flip-flops."

She smiled and grabbed her stuff and headed into the bathroom. She hung up her garment bag with Gram's dress and veil. Wrapped up inside were a pair of peau de soie peep-toe pumps that Clementine had had to buy once as a bridesmaid. Luckily they wore the same size shoe.

Something old: Gram's dress and veil.

Something new: the lacy bra and panties she'd bought in Dallas but had never worn.

Something borrowed: Clementine's shoes.

Something blue: her mother's diamond and sapphire bracelet.

She slipped out of her clothes and into the fancy lingerie, then put on the beautiful paper-thin lace dress, like something Grace Kelly or Audrey Hepburn might have worn. It was tea-length and sleeveless and so beautiful that Annabel almost burst into tears. Her grandmother had married the love of her life in this dress fifty years ago.

Annabel was marrying the right man, in the right dress, for sensible reasons. She slid the veil on and fluffed it back and almost cried again. She looked like a bride.

She wished her gram and her sisters and her parents were here. She'd promised Clementine behind-the-scenes pictures, so she snapped a couple of selfies, which was so silly it made her smile. A light dusting of makeup, a spritz of Chanel No 19, the bracelet and shoes on and she was ready.

When she opened the door and stepped out, West stared at her—hard.

"Oh my God, Annabel. You look absolutely beautiful. Too beautiful."

She managed a smile, afraid to get all choked up and end up with mascara tracks down her cheeks.

"Let's go get married," West said.

When the officiant called their names, Annabel looped her arm through West's and headed into the small chapel. A narrow red velvet carpet, appropriate, since Annabel did feel a bit like an actress, led from the door to where the officiant stood in front of a stained glass window—church effect, Annabel supposed—and an arrangement of exquisite red roses. The officiant, a woman in her fifties, wearing a mint-green suit and veiled hat, introduced Annabel and West to their witnesses, since they brought none of their own, a couple whose job it was to attend quickie weddings, sign licenses and snap photos.

Annabel stood across from West, glancing around as he was doing. She got it. It wasn't easy to stand across from the person you were vowing to love, honor and cherish till death did you part when those vows were actually about something else. *Annabel: I vow to make healthful breakfasts for your daughter, make sure her hair is knot-free and weed her closet of raggedy, holey pants. West: I vow to keep Hurley's Homestyle Kitchen afloat.*

The officiant called for the rings, which until this moment Annabel had completely overlooked. But West pulled two rings out of his pocket, a plain gold band and a beautiful gold band dotted with diamonds. He must have bought them before they arrived.

"Do you take this woman to be your lawfully wedded wife?" the officiant asked West, nothing about vowing to love or cherish her.

West took Annabel's left hand in his, sliding the stunning diamond band halfway on her finger. He cleared his throat. "I do." He slid the ring the rest of the way. It fit perfectly, which meant he must have asked Clementine for her ring size.

Annabel tried to hold West's gaze, but she glanced

at her ring, then at her peau de soie shoes and tried to breathe.

West handed Annabel his ring and held out his hand. She took the ring and slid it halfway up his ring finger.

"And do you, Annabel Hurley, take this man, Weston Dallas Montgomery, to be your lawfully wedded husband?"

She hadn't known his middle name was Dallas. She was marrying a man, right this moment, whose middle name she hadn't known.

She looked into West's driftwood-colored eyes, intense and soft on her at the same time, and part of her wanted to shout, *Of course I do! He's West Montgomery.* But the rest of her knew that he wasn't marrying her because he loved her, and standing here, actually marrying him, felt terribly wrong. So wrong that her stomach turned over and tears pricked the backs of her eyes. She looked down, blinking the tears away.

"Annabel? You okay?" West whispered.

"Just a little overwhelmed with emotion," she managed to squeak out. She glanced at the officiant, then at West. "I do. I do take this man." She slid the ring fully on his finger.

He kept his eyes on hers and nodded, giving her hand a little squeeze.

"I now pronounce you husband and wife," the officiant said. "You may now kiss the bride."

West leaned over, taking her face in his hands, and kissed her—passionately. Annabel leaned into him, kissing him back, feeling herself swoon. There was nothing fake, nothing temporary, nothing businesslike about the kiss. It showed his passionate appreciation, she realized. But then it was over, West pulling back.

The witnesses took lots of pictures with West's and Annabel's phones, and West sent a couple of shots right away to Lucy, via the Dunkins' email since she was staying with them for the night. Then the officiant called for the four-thirty couple, and Mr. and Mrs. Montgomery found themselves outside the chapel.

A limo passed them, a woman flashing her breasts and drunkenly shouting, "Whoo-hoo! Vegas, baby!" out the window. Up and down the Strip, Annabel could see a few brides in all different kinds of gowns, one groom in a New England Patriots jersey and helmet. "So, Mrs. Annabel Hurley Montgomery, for your wedding night, would you like a wild night on the town or quiet room service on the balcony, just the two of us?"

"Which would you prefer?" she asked, hoping he'd go for door number two.

"Just the two of us."

"Me too," she said.

They walked back to their hotel, just a short distance away, folks congratulating them along the way.

But all the way up in the elevator to the seventeenth floor, she kept thinking about how they hadn't ironed out the sex issue. Was West expecting a real wedding night? Was she? Was it better not to start something she wasn't sure should continue? Would sex complicate what was a temporary business arrangement?

What didn't sex complicate?

But as West stood so close beside her, all six feet three inches of him, the delicious clean soap smell of him, she saw herself beneath him in the hayloft, the guy of her dreams, now her legal husband. Her *husband*. She wanted him—desperately.

* * *

On the balcony, West took a few selfies of the two of them holding up their rings. Then room service arrived, and they decided to get out of their fancy clothes before eating. West headed into the bathroom with his overnight bag and returned wearing a pair of very sexy jeans and a navy blue T-shirt. Annabel grabbed her own bag and shot inside, closing the door and sucking in a deep breath. She carefully removed her dress and hung it back in the garment bag with the shoes and veil, then changed into skinny jeans and a ruffly white tank top, leaving her hair loose.

For a second she was about to slide off the ring but realized it was meant to stay on. She stared at it, wondering how long it would take to feel comfortable on her finger, to feel as though it belonged.

She found West on the balcony, pouring two glasses of champagne. He handed her one, then held his own up to her.

"To you," he said. "If it weren't for you…" He glanced away, down at the sparkling lights of the Strip, then cleared his throat. "Sometimes I can't believe that we really had to resort to such a drastic measure."

Sometimes Annabel thought West shouldn't talk so much.

"I mean, I really thought I was done with marriage," he went on. "Once burned, twice shy and all that." He sat down at the little round table on the balcony, removing the lid on his dinner: prime rib, classic wedding entrée.

"How were you burned?" she asked, realizing she knew very little about his marriage to Lorna. She removed the lid on hers, not much appetite for the delicious-looking lemon sole.

"Maybe we should have our toast first," he said, clinking her glass. "To…this marriage doing its job."

Good Lord. The less he talked the better. Annabel wondered if the room service menu had earplugs.

It wasn't that she didn't understand that this was a business deal, a temporary one, at that. But they were legally, lawfully wed, husband and wife, and they'd be sharing a home, a bedroom, acting in public like a happy married couple. He could at least…something. Ugh. This was so frustrating. Although…did she want him to pretend to love her? Of course not.

He sliced into his prime rib. "I married Lorna because she was pregnant. To be honest, at the time, I didn't even like her. But she told me she was pregnant with my baby, so I proposed marriage. You know what her answer was? 'If you can get me the two-carat ring I want from Blue Gulch Jewelers, size six, okay, I'll marry you.' I sold my one and only head of cattle, and I bought her the ring she wanted."

"So she wouldn't have married you if you didn't buy her that ring?"

West laughed. "Honestly I don't know."

"You said 'at the time' you didn't like her. Things changed between you?"

If things changed for the better with him and Lorna, maybe there was hope that things could change for them. Maybe.

"She had her good points," he said, biting off the head of a stalk of asparagus. "Very soon after Lorna told me she was pregnant, my parents moved to Austin and said I could have the house and their small herd of cattle. A wedding present, I guess. Lorna hated the idea, but it was either that or moving in with her folks, and she thought living on a ranch might be fun."

Annabel tried to imagine Lorna Dunkin on a ranch with her three-inch heels.

West looked down at the lights of the Strip, waiting for a limo beeping to the tune of the Wedding March to pipe down. At least it made them both smile. "Anyway, for most of her pregnancy, Lorna did seem to like it okay. But she got sick of it. Right before she was due, she wanted to move to town, which I couldn't afford. And my parents had died just a few months before that. There was no way I was selling my family homestead with my brother and my parents both gone. The house, the land were the only things I had left of my family, even if we didn't get along."

"I can understand that," she said. "When my parents died it was hard to leave the house we grew up in and move to Gram's Victorian. Clementine took that the hardest." Annabel thought of Clem, having shuffled from foster home to foster home, losing the adoptive parents she thought would be her forever family.

West nodded. "Then when Lucy was born, I was so madly in love with that little six-pound baby that I desperately wanted things to work out between Lorna and me. She could be fun, had a good sense of humor, liked to have a good time. And here and there, she'd dote on Lucy. But she hated the ranch, wanted to go out with her girlfriends, starting staying in town more and more instead of coming home at night. I tried to make her happy any way I could to keep her home for Lucy's sake, but a year ago, right before the accident, she told me she couldn't take another minute of her life, she loved Lucy but she couldn't be a good mother if she was miserable, so she was taking off for New York City to try to become a singer." He shook his head. "Can you imagine just leaving your kid?"

"No. I really can't." It was unfathomable.

He took a swig of champagne. "In that moment, when Lorna told me she was leaving Lucy—a five-year-old—any feelings I had for my wife turned to ash."

She didn't know what to say, so she sipped her own champagne, her appetite totally gone.

"At least now I know what I'm dealing with," he said, holding up his left hand, the gold band glinting with the sunset. "Believe me, I prefer this. We know exactly what we are doing here, how you feel, how I feel."

"Oh?" she said before she could stop herself. "How do I feel?"

He looked up at her, tilting his head. "You feel like saving Hurley's means the world to you. That you'd do anything for your gram, anything to save the family business. And you're doing it—you married a man you barely know, a man you don't love, a man you probably don't even like." He dropped his head for a moment. "When I look back on how we left things seven years ago, I'd expect you to hate me, actually."

She both wanted to talk about this and didn't want to talk about this. She breathed in deeply, the scent of her bridal bouquet on a little table nearby reaching her.

"I don't hate you," she said. "Obviously," she added, managing a small smile.

"I suppose. Or all the money in the world wouldn't have made you marry me."

She wanted to tell him that she hadn't married him for money at all, that she would have said her *I do* anyway, to help him keep his daughter. But right now it was her only protection, the only thing that kept her from feeling entirely vulnerable.

"I am sorry," he said. "For what I did to you seven years ago. I shouldn't have just left it like that, never talked to you about it."

"That was a long time ago. A lifetime ago, really." For him anyway. He'd married, had a child, been widowed, become a prosperous rancher. She stood up and braced her hands on the railing, watching the people below, the sparkling lights. But she'd always wanted to know why he'd stopped so suddenly that night in the hayloft. "What happened that night?" she asked softly, facing the Strip.

He stood up and moved beside her, resting his forearms on the rail. "I knew I was taking advantage of you, so I stopped."

She whirled to face him. "What?"

"I was half out of my mind that night, Annabel. I'd just lost my brother. My parents, my family, were all ignoring me because I was the black-sheep kid, the bad seed, the troublemaker, and they didn't say it, but I knew they were thinking, 'Too bad it wasn't West.'"

Her heart constricted for him. How awful to believe that was what his own parents had been thinking. "What? No. No one thought that, West." She put her hand on his arm.

He stiffened, and she pulled her hand away. "Like you said, Annabel, it was a long time ago."

She knew she should change the subject from his parents. "You weren't taking advantage of me, by the way. I was there very willingly."

"I know, but I doubt you wanted to go from what—

the first time we'd ever really had a conversation to sex. You were there, you were beautiful and I couldn't keep my hands off you. I didn't want to take advantage of that."

You were beautiful... "I've always thought it was the grief that made you reach for me," she said. "I mean, I was Geekabel with my container of chili and you were... West Montgomery."

He raised an eyebrow. "Geekabel?"

"Some girls at school liked to call me that," she said. "I guess I thought that's how you looked at me too."

From the look in his eyes, he clearly had no idea what she was talking about. "All I know is that the beautiful, tall, auburn-haired girl I'd see around town, working at Hurley's, was in the hayloft with me, talking to me the way no one ever had, listening like what I had to say mattered, meant something. I wanted you so badly that night. And when you let me take off your shirt and I saw that lacy bra, I couldn't control myself and was all over you."

She remembered.

"But then there was this moment that I stared into your eyes, and you looked so trusting, so innocent, and I called myself a jerk and made myself stop."

"Oh, West," she said, putting her hand back on his arm.

He turned and pulled her close, his mouth coming down hard on hers. She closed her eyes and arched into him, wrapping her arms around his neck. He picked her up—and at five foot nine, Annabel was a tall woman—and effortlessly carried her into the room and laid her down on the bed, then lay down on top of her, moving her arms up on either side of her head and holding them there while he kissed her hard and possessively.

He released her hands and she tangled them in his hair as his own hands inched up under her top, roaming over her bra, her stomach, the snap of her jeans, which he undid in a split second, the denim sliding down her hips and legs and feet until they were in a heap on the floor. He leaned up and looked down the length of her, sliding a finger under the narrow lacy band of her fancy ivory silk panties and inching them down her legs. She closed her eyes, aware of nothing but her heartbeat, the scent of his soap, the sensations building inside her. West moved and she opened her eyes to find him sitting at the edge of the bed, removing his T-shirt, then his own jeans and finally his underwear.

He lay down on top of her again, her arms back over her head as he kissed her neck and collarbone, then her ear, one hand freeing to slide down her shoulder, her stomach. Suddenly his hands, his mouth, were moving upward, his fingers reaching behind her to unclasp the matching little bra and letting it drop on the floor. Then his mouth explored her breasts, back up to her neck and her lips. She wanted to touch him, to run her own hands all over his body, but she held back, feeling a little shy.

"I can't wait another second," he whispered, reaching across the bed to the table, the crackle sound of a condom wrapper opening no match for how loudly her heart was beating. "You're so beautiful, Annabel," he said and then he was inside her, and Annabel gasped with how incredibly good it felt, how at home she was with him, how much she loved this man. Her husband.

When West woke up, Annabel naked and sleeping beside him, a long tangle of her auburn hair across her cheek, he had the strongest urge to wrap her in his arms and slowly wake her up by trailing kisses down her stomach. But as he looked at her, so peaceful, so innocent, he cursed himself for not only taking advantage of her again—but losing control completely and making love to her. How many glasses of champagne had they had? Barely one glass each. He couldn't even blame it on booze. Their marriage was a business deal, and to complicate it with sex was a huge mistake. One of them would end up hurt, and to be honest, he wasn't sure which of them it would be.

As he watched Annabel sleep, he heard his parents' voices… *If her grandmother had any sense she'd send Annabel away tomorrow... I love West...but he is who he is*.

If only they knew. She *had* gotten away from him and now he'd dragged her into his mess.

He felt something shutter inside him and turned away, getting out of bed. The last time he'd been incommunicado for his daughter because he'd been in bed with a woman, he'd vowed no more women. That he'd focus all his emotional energy on his daughter. Now, because of his uncontrollable lust for Annabel and the emotion of the day—his own wedding—he'd gone too far. Bad for Annabel and bad for him. And bad for Lucy. He had to remember he'd gotten married for Lucy. She was his focus.

So that was that. He'd keep his distance— physically *and* emotionally. In three, six, twelve months—however long it took for him to learn how to be a father to the point that he could do it on his own—Annabel would leave, start her own life. She deserved that. Not some faux husband who'd take advantage of their sharing a bedroom while she was around.

Jerk.

West glanced at the wall of windows, no idea what time it was. The Vegas hotel blackout curtains did a good job of keeping the room dark for revelers and gamblers to sleep late after a night on the Strip. He picked up his jeans from the floor and reached for his phone in his back pocket. It was barely six in the morning. Their flight was at ten.

He glanced at Annabel. It took everything in him not to get back into bed, to drag his gaze away from her curvy figure under the blanket, from her beautiful face. *She's not your wife*, he reminded himself. *Not really.*

But today was the first full day of their marriage, and he was going to do this right. Which meant getting the hell out of the room before he couldn't control himself.

Chapter Seven

The first thing Annabel saw when she opened her eyes in the morning was her wedding ring, the beautiful diamond band glittering on her finger, her hand lying over West's pillow. The second thing was the note where West's head should be.

Annabel sat up and snatched the note, written on hotel stationery. *A—Loading up the car. I'll be back with breakfast.—W*

Loading up the car with two garment bags and two overnight bags? She could have carried those down herself with one hand. Well, two, but still. There was only one reason why a man would leave a hotel room where a naked woman was sleeping. To get away.

She dropped the note and pulled her knees up under her chin, staring out the window at what she could see through the filmy white curtains, the heavy dark drapes pulled to the sides. The sky was overcast, perfect for her mood. No sunshine here.

Then again, maybe she was misreading things. Maybe West had woken up, didn't want to wake her and was being thoughtful by bringing down the bags and picking up breakfast. But not even very deep down she knew that wasn't the case. First of all, he'd meant to wake her, because he'd opened the drapes. Second, had *she* woken up before West, she would have watched him sleep, sighing inwardly in contentment, and waited for his eyes to open so she could feel those lips on her again. West woke up and left.

As Yogi Berra once said, "It was déjà vu all over again." Well, sort of. It wasn't as if this time he could run into the arms of another woman; they were married, and as West had brilliantly put it, their marriage had a job to do. In fact, keeping the relationship "professional" was key. They'd gotten married yesterday, legally married, had some champagne and gotten carried away. The bright light of day and reality must have had its way with West when he woke up. *Nothing to get all up in arms about, Annabel. This isn't a real marriage.* She chanted it three times, feeling as though she could click her heels three times too and she'd end up back in Hurley's in the kitchen.

She heard the card key click open the door and she pulled the blanket up higher on her chest. West appeared, a white paper bag in his hand. "Oh, you're…not dressed. I'll go set up breakfast and give you a chance to take a quick shower. Our flight's at just before ten, so we have about an hour and a half before we need to leave."

He'd moved to the suite area, so she couldn't see

him; she could only hear him going on, his voice a bit strained and too bright, as if he was fighting with himself to be…lighthearted.

She pulled out the sheet and wrapped it around herself and darted past him into the bathroom, turning on the shower fast in case she burst into tears. Sex complicated things. Hadn't he said that? She knew what this marriage was about. He wasn't her husband. She was his temporary wife. She was temporary stepmother to his daughter.

By the time she came out of the shower and was dressed in a T-shirt, jeans, flip-flops and her favorite thick cardigan, Annabel's head was on straight.

Except when she left the bathroom and found West sitting at the little round table on the balcony, two coffees, two breakfast sandwiches and two oranges in front of him, her heart pinged in her chest with how much she really did love him. *You'd better be careful*, she warned herself as she pasted a smile on her face. *You think you got hurt seven years ago? You ain't seen nothing yet.*

He was watching her, she realized, taking stock of what she thought about his leaving her alone in bed.

Cut him a break, she ordered herself. *Give him what he needs and remember why he married you in the first place.* "I'm really excited to sit down with some of the business initiatives I've been working on for Hurley's and get those into place," she said, adding cream and sugar to her coffee. "Team Hurley's," she added, holding up a palm for a high five like a total moron.

He glanced at her, nodded and high-fived her. "Team Hurley's." He gave her a tight smile and picked up his bacon and egg on an English muffin and glanced down at the Strip. He said something about the weather, then talked about how much he missed Lucy, that he hated nights away from her, even when she was just a few miles away in town at her grandparents'. For a couple of minutes he was silent and seemed lost in thought.

"So I've been thinking," he said, taking another slug of his coffee. "Last night, the champagne clearly got the better of me. It's probably best if we…don't complicate things. Do you agree?"

"Of course," she said, taking a bite of her breakfast sandwich to show how completely okay she was with the conversation. She could barely choke down the bite, her stomach twisting. "I completely agree. Like you said last night, our marriage has a job to do. Let's let it do that job." That was her new motto. As long as she kept saying it over and over in her head, she'd stay sane.

Suddenly they were doing this weird "polite" thing with each other, West thought as they exited the plane and followed the crowds to Baggage Claim and the exit in the Austin Airport. All through the almost-three-hour flight, it was *No, you take the window seat.* They both sat ramrod straight, not letting their thighs touch, neither taking their shared arm rest. Good Lord, it was exhausting.

And he couldn't stop staring at their rings. He'd taken his first wedding ring off a few weeks after Lorna died, and the look her mother had given him when she noticed could have frozen lava. He'd overheard Raina telling her husband that it was the ultimate sign of disrespect, that West would probably be out carousing with God knew what trampy women who would mistreat Lucy. Normally West would have seethed inwardly and moved on, but he'd sat the Dunkins down right then and there and had told them that taking off the ring wasn't about his feelings for Lorna or letting single women know he was free. It was about accepting that Lucy's mother was gone, that his life and Lucy's had irrevocably changed and he was trying to adjust to their lives without her. Raina had burst into tears, her husband comforting her and waving West away.

Even when he thought he said the right things, they turned out to be wrong. So a man who was never much for expressing how he felt clammed up even tighter. Except when it came to Lucy. No matter how hard it was sometimes, he wanted her to talk about everything, including her mother, and not feel she couldn't talk about her loss with him. Especially because for some reason, whenever Lucy brought up her mother with Raina, the woman would change the subject. Maybe it was too painful for Raina. Hell, it was painful for West. But Lucy had to be able to talk about her mother, no matter what.

Annabel was quiet the hour's drive from the airport to Blue Gulch. If he were honest, he'd admit that he didn't really want to know what she was thinking. Because it probably had to do with his loss of control last night, mucking things up between them by being unable to resist her. Or maybe she was thinking about giving up a chunk of her life to marry him. *Our marriage has a job to do.* He liked chanting it in his head as a reminder of the truth, that Annabel wasn't his, that she hadn't married him for any other reason than to save her family's business.

As they headed into the center of town, West turned off Blue Gulch Street toward the ranch, hoping that

Lottie remembered to feed Daisy this morning as she'd promised.

Annabel sat up straight in her seat and glanced back toward the main road. "Aren't you going to drop me off at my house?"

He glanced at her. "Your house is now my house, remember?"

She looked at the dashboard clock. "But I could help with the dinner prep. My Creole sauce for the po'boys got raves the past few days and I want to keep customers—"

West pulled over. "When you said earlier that you were glad you'd be home in time for dinner prep, I thought you meant at my house—*our* house. For Lucy."

"Well, of course I'll make a healthy dinner for you and Lucy—at dinnertime. But Hurley's—"

"I told you I'd take care of Hurley's. Your main concern right now is keeping the Dunkins satisfied that Lucy is being raised 'right,' aka *their* way."

She glared at him. "I'm not saying a restaurant is more important than a child, West. Or a family. But Hurley's Homestyle Kitchen *is* my family. And therefore it is equally important to me. I'm not going to shirk my responsibilities to the restaurant, to my gram, just because you're throwing money at the place."

A muscle worked overtime in his temple. "I guess there are a few things we didn't iron out before we got married."

Like sex. They should have talked about that, not left it "for later discussion." Now every time he looked at Annabel he saw her naked and breathless and wanting more of him. He closed his eyes for a moment to get the image out of his head. As if that were possible.

Keep your head in this conversation, he ordered himself.

He turned to face her, his arms crossed over his chest. "Well, hell, Annabel, it's not like you can be in Hurley's kitchen for the dinner rush anymore. I need you at my house, making grilled chicken and asparagus and combing the tangles out of Lucy's hair after her bath. That's your main job now."

The glare was back. "Yes, I know. But as you have made perfectly clear, West, this is a temporary marriage. The point is to get your house up to snuff for the Dunkins, right? You're going to have to learn to do this yourself so that when I leave, they're not hauling you into court. Rely on me, yes. But not to the exclusion of you learning what needs to be done—even if it's just for the Dunkins' sake."

She had a point. "But look at where trying got me. I still can't cook. I can't get the knots out of Lucy's hair or make it look like Lorna used to. And I always think she looks adorable, especially with green tights and bright shirts and orange skirts. I need you, Annabel."

Her expression softened. "You need me to help you learn some aspects of fatherhood that don't come easily to you. But you'll learn, West. And you'll be great at it. Don't you know the key to any success is motivation? You've got that by the truckload."

He stared at the steering wheel, the conversation having gotten away from him somehow. "So you're not going to be home at dinnertime? You're not going to help Lucy with her bath?"

She was quiet for a moment. "I guess we forgot to sit down and talk about our expectations for the marriage. We have a few hours before Lucy gets home from school. Let's go to the ranch and set the ground rules."

He sighed. Loudly.

This was home now, Annabel thought, watching West give Daisy the beagle a vigorous petting and then check in with his two hands who were working in the open barn. He waved Annabel over and introduced her to Jonas and PJ, both in their early twenties. Jonas reported that one of the calves' legs was better this morning, and after a bit of talking about what needed tending to today, the cowboys nodded at her and headed farther into the barn.

"Was it strange, introducing me as your wife?" Annabel asked as they walked toward the pickup to get their bags. Then she wished she could take it back. Of course it was strange. *Stop saying everything in your head*, she ordered herself. Bad habit.

"It'll take some getting used to," he said, grabbing the bags and leading the way into the house.

Tell me about it, she thought. *You know West, my husband*, she imagined saying to the librarian as they'd go into the children's section with Lucy. *Let me just tell my husband I'll be a minute. My husband thinks... My husband said... My husband and I...* A long-ago dream that had become a reality. Temporarily.

"I'll bring these up to our room," he said, and she watched him head up the stairs. *Our room.*

Needing to orient herself in her own world, she said, "I'll call Clementine and see how things are at the restaurant."

She walked through the living room, taking in the furnishings, Lucy's easel and toy chest by the window.

The place was comfortable and warm and a real home. There were "feminine" touches everywhere, so either West had left things as Lorna had decorated or he'd done a good job on that front himself. There were lots of photos of Lucy on tables and the mantel. She picked one up, of West with Lucy on his shoulders at a parade. Judging by the little American flag in Lucy's hand, waved high over her head, Annabel figured it had been taken at last year's Fourth of July parade. West was smiling, and the look on Lucy's face was priceless, a big sneaky grin.

"I'll make sure you two are never separated," she said to the photo.

She heard West's feet on the steps, so she walked into the kitchen and out the back door with her phone. The fresh country air, the scent of hay and horses mingling, was refreshing. She was pretty sure she'd like farm life just fine. She stood against a wooden fence, watching a herd of cattle graze in the pasture, as she waited for Clementine to pick up.

"Annabel, don't even think about coming in today," her sister said. "You had what—a one-night honeymoon? Take the weekend off, at least. And besides, now that Gram's hired Martha full-time and word's spread that she's in charge of the ribs, we actually got five reservations for tonight. The last time someone made reservations for a Saturday night was months ago."

Martha Perkins, beloved in town, used to work for Gram as her full-time assistant cook, but then the woman had moved to Austin to help her daughter with her new triplets. Apparently Martha was so happy to be able to come back home to Blue Gulch that she accepted Gram's offer.

"But how could Gram have afforded to hire—" Duh, Annabel thought. West.

"Apparently, when Gram had her little chat with West on Friday, he said that his money was our money now that we were going to be a family, and therefore, he'd stocked the business account with enough money to take care of whatever needed taking care of. He told Gram and me to do whatever we felt was necessary to turn Hurley's around. Gram got on the phone and now Martha's starting at Hurley's tonight. So we'd better not see your face yet," Clementine added. "Between Hattie, Harold and Martha working tonight and brunch and dinner tomorrow, and then with us closed Monday, I'd say we'll see you Tuesday at the earliest. So go enjoy your new husband."

If only I could, Annabel thought, saying goodbye to Clementine and pocketing her phone.

She went back inside and found West in the kitchen, adding water to the coffee maker.

"So you've already funded Gram's business account," she said. "That was fast."

"Necessary on several counts," he said. "The sooner you all can focus on improvements versus just staying afloat, the sooner you'll be back in the black."

"And this way I can focus my attention on my part of the bargain," she said, her back getting up about his steamroller ways. But he'd kept his part of the deal and then some. Okay, she got it. She still wanted to be part of Hurley's day to day, but she didn't have to be in the kitchen to do that; she needed to manage the restaurant, even if that wasn't her forte, and by having the best cooks besides her gram in the kitchen, Annabel could focus on running the restaurant.

He nodded. "Look, I know Hurley's is important to you. And everything's in place to build it back up. Right now everything with the Dunkins is urgent. We need to show them Lucy will be taken care of to their liking. Or they'll drag me into court and they could very well win."

"So let's talk about my schedule," she said, sitting down at the table. "And exactly what my responsibilities will be." How could she not have thought about what would be required day to day? She'd been so focused on West that she'd forgotten to think about how her days and nights would be structured. For the most part, she knew, West had hired her to be a very good stepmother.

He brewed a pot of coffee. "As far as Hurley's goes, I understand that you don't want to take a passive role even if there's money in the account now. So how about if you work the lunch shift—whether cooking or taking on more of a managerial role?"

Just what she'd been thinking. "I'd been hoping my sister Georgia would come home and take that on," she said. "But something's keeping her in Houston. So I guess I'd better accept that I need to run Hurley's." She got up to pour the coffee and bring out the mugs, cream and sugar. She might as well start also accepting that she lived here now; she wasn't a guest. She'd bring her favorite purple mug. That would help. And the chocolatey coffee they served at Hurley's. West either liked his coffee bitter or had just gotten used to it.

He took a long slug of his coffee. "Thanks. I needed that." One more long swallow and he put the mug down. "And now that staffing has been increased, you can be home to greet Lucy off the bus at three-twenty, and I won't need to rely on Dottie, Lucy's sitter, so much."

She stirred extra cream and sugar into her own mug. "Okay, so I'll meet Lucy at the bus stop at three-twenty and then my focus will be on her—homework, snack, playing, making dinner, bath, getting her ready for bedtime, laying out clothes for the next school day."

He nodded. "And dealing with the Dunkins, starting tomorrow night at dinner at their house. They're keeping Lucy until then. Their wedding present to us, Raina said."

He glanced at her—uneasily, Annabel thought. They'd be alone again tonight.

Annabel had been hoping to get started on learning how to be a stepmother right away. And yes, having a little girl in the house would have given Annabel something to do, something to focus on. Now all she had in her head was how tonight was going to work, the elephant in the middle of the room again, aka West's bed. Their bed.

"I suppose we should act like newlyweds when we're at the Dunkins'," Annabel said. "Instead of almost strangers."

"We're hardly strangers. I've seen you naked." He slid a smile at her, and she could tell he was trying to diffuse the tension, not just between them but about the show they'd have to put on for Lucy's grandparents.

She felt her cheeks redden. "What if they can tell… I mean, that we're faking it?"

He took her hand and held it. "I thought about that. And you know what? I'm not faking how grateful I am to you for saving my life. How much I appreciate what you've given up to do this."

Annabel looked at him, confused. "What have I given up?"

He released her hand to pick up his mug. "A relationship with someone you want to be with. Like I said last night, I know I'm not high on your favorite-people list."

Now wasn't the time or place to bring up seven years ago again, why he'd really dumped her for Lorna. Fine, he thought he was taking advantage of her so he'd called a halt to what was going on between them in the hayloft. But that didn't explain continuing it with Lorna Dunkin the next day, in the very spot she'd found him crying, where they'd spoken for the first time, where the guy she'd secretly loved for years had let her hug him at the news that his older brother had died overseas, the IED also destroying his parents, their family.

She let out a breath. "I admire how far you're willing to go to keep your daughter. That you care about her that much says quite a lot."

He looked at her for a long moment, then nodded. "So we like each other," he finally said. "We admire things about the other. The Dunkins won't have reason to think we're not a very happily married couple. No one expects us to start groping each other at dinner with grandparents at the table."

She laughed. "I suppose not."

"So we'll be fine."

Ha. She'd have to get through tonight first.

It was only five o'clock. How to pass the next six or so hours?

It took West a while to catch on, but he finally realized that Annabel had been using stalling tactics all night to avoid their bedroom. She'd cleaned the kitchen until it shone, then brought up cleaning supplies to Lucy's bathroom and spent a good twenty minutes scraping goop off the cap of her bubble-fruit tooth-paste. Then she straightened the books on the living room bookshelves, politely smiling with a nod every time he passed through the room she was in.

At just after one, when he came in from checking on a calf who'd been having problems with his hind leg, West found Annabel fast asleep on the couch, the book *How to Talk So Kids Will Listen* facedown on her stom-ach, and a feather duster under her hand.

He gently scooped her up in his arms and carried her into the bedroom, trying to avoid smelling the light perfume she always wore. How could someone who'd scrubbed rooms for the past few hours look and smell so incredibly sexy?

He laid her down in the bed and spread a blanket over her, wanting to lie down beside her. But given that they were alone, there was no good reason for him to sleep next to her.

He thought about what tomorrow night would be like, showing up at the Dunkins with his wife by his side and feeling for the first time in days like ten linebac-kers weren't sitting on his chest. That terrible pressure was gone. A strange burst of feeling rose in him, but he wasn't sure if it was gratitude or something more, some-thing he couldn't put his finger on. God, how he wanted to slide his hands beneath her and pull Annabel into his arms and hold her, just hold her tightly against him.

It took everything in him to quietly leave, shutting the door behind him—just as he'd done this morning.

Chapter Eight

The Dunkins lived in a stately Colonial just off Blue Gulch Street in the center of town. As Annabel walked beside West up the stone path, he took her hand and smiled at her—a commiserating smile, she realized. Sometimes, such as right then, she felt such a kinship with him, them against the world—well, the Dunkins. Other times, like this morning, when she'd woken up alone in West's bed—her bed, she amended—she felt so separate from him, so aware of their arrangement and how far apart they truly were.

West must have been doing morning rounds when she woke this morning, so she'd left him a note to let him know she'd gone back to the apricot Victorian to pack a suitcase's worth of clothes, though if she'd been honest, she'd have added that she needed to be back on her own turf for a little while. Last night, after a cleaning frenzy, she'd found a parenting book on the book-shelf and had started reading it on the couch, but West must have found her asleep and carried her up to bed… then left. Part of her knew his leaving was for the best, and without Lucy home, there'd been no good reason for him to have stayed in the room with her. But another part of her wanted him to want to, to want her the way he did on their wedding night.

At the family home, Gram had been sleeping, and Clementine had been full of questions about the wedding, which Annabel answered honestly, and then Clementine had helped her choose the right outfit to officially "meet" her stepdaughter's maternal grandparents. They shook their heads at the jeans and shorts in her closet and went for the "Dallas clothes," a suitcase Annabel hadn't even bothered to unpack yet. A cute, flippy yellow eyelet skirt with a sleeveless, ruffly white top and silver ballet slippers. The tiny gold starfish necklace her mother had given her for Christmas when she was twelve and gold hoop earrings from her dad. Back at the ranch, when she came out of the bedroom, hair brushed and shiny, light dusting of makeup, West had told her how grateful he was that she "got" the Dunkins. She took that to mean he thought Raina would approve of how she looked.

West rang the bell. Raina opened the door and ignored West and took both of Annabel's hands in hers. Across the living room, through the sliding glass doors to the backyard, Annabel could see Lucy playing outside with her grandfather, and West hurried to the back door to see his daughter.

Raina was beaming, her ash-blond hair in a stylish bob with long, side-swept bangs. She wore a pale yellow peplum top with matching silk capris and high-heeled sandals and several sparkling bracelets. "Annabel, I'm so thrilled that you're our Lucy's new stepmama. I just know she's going to be in such good hands now."

"Thank you, Mrs. Dunkin, but—"

Raina wagged a finger, her hazel eyes warm. "We're practically family now. Call me Raina."

"Raina." Annabel smiled. "And Lucy has always been in good hands."

Raina let out a burst of laughter. "Oh my, you *are* in love." She laughed again as if what Annabel had said was beyond ridiculous. "We're having just a simple Sunday dinner, Landon's Cornish hens, my famous scalloped potatoes and green beans. Of course, we're no match for a Dallas chef—I heard you were working at Table 44, which I know is a Michelin-starred restaurant."

Annabel didn't really want to be reminded about Dallas, where she'd been nothing but lonely. "Well, these days I'm all about barbecue sauce and coleslaw—and that's always been more my style."

"My dear, life is about family. And Hurley's is a Blue Gulch institution. Be proud of being reared on that sauce and slaw. Did you know I had my first date at Hurley's? Twenty-eight years ago." She smiled and sighed. "I have good memories of that place."

"Me too," Annabel said, reminded that West was saving Hurley's for everyone, not just her family. She glanced at Raina, surprised she was warmer and friendlier than Annabel expected and actually kind of likeable.

"Annabel!" came a happy little voice as a whirlwind rushed in and wrapped her arms around Annabel's hips.

West laughed as he came in the room, Landon Dunkin behind him. Landon wrapped Annabel in a hug and welcomed her to his home.

"Lucy," Raina admonished. "Is that how a little lady greets someone?"

"Yes!" Lucy said, and giggled. At Raina's raised eyebrow, Lucy turned to Annabel and said, "Hi!"

Annabel kneeled down and gave Lucy a hug. "Hi, Lucy!"

"Want to see my room here at Nana and Pop-Pop's house?" Lucy asked, pulling Annabel down the hall.

As Annabel headed into the very pink, very frilly room fit for a princess, she was aware of the silence coming from the living room. A strained silence. She could imagine West standing there with the Dunkins, staring at nothing in particular, waiting for Annabel and Lucy to return. She heard Landon say, "Well, let me go check on my roast." A moment later, Raina told West to make himself comfortable while she finished up the salad. Then there was the clicking of Raina's heels on the hardwood floor.

Lucy showed Annabel her bookcase with her porcelain doll collection, then the dolls she was allowed to play with. Stark difference between this room and West's living room with the LEGO structures, action figures, dolls and superheroes. Holding a rag doll with bright red hair, Lucy titled her head and said, "Are you my stepmother now?"

Annabel smiled. "I am. And I'm very happy about that."

"Me too," Lucy said, holding the doll to her chest. "I miss my mommy, but I'm happy about having a nice stepmother."

"I miss my mom too," Annabel said, and gave Lucy's hand a gentle squeeze. "If you ever need to talk about how it feels to miss your mother, you can always talk to me if you want."

Lucy nodded sagely and put the doll back on the shelf. Then Raina's voice called out that it was time for dinner, so Lucy led the way into the living room.

"How about we both wash our hands before we sit down at the table to eat?" Annabel said, smiling at Lucy as they entered the living room.

"Just down the hall, dear," Raina said with a satisfied smile.

Annabel caught the equally satisfied look on West's face.

Well, if Annabel had been worried about "fooling" anyone about the state of her and West's marriage, she could certainly relax. Perhaps this was really about appearances, as West had said, and all that mattered was making the right noises and giving the right directives. *Wash your hands, say please and thank you, remember your manners.*

A few minutes later, they were all seated, the Dunkins at the head of the rectangular table in the formal dining room, West and Annabel on one side, Lucy on the other. Dinner passed with the usual small talk, the weather, which specials at Hurley's most people liked best, the secret in the Creole sauce, how Annabel's sisters were doing; Raina had commented that Georgia would surely come home to see about her grandmother, and Annabel said she was expected soon. Then there was some talk about baseball and how the Texas Rangers had fared this season, how many calves West was preparing for auction, and lots of talk about Lucy's school and teacher, Ms. Johnson, and that Lucy was starting to read chapter books.

Twice Lucy had mentioned her mother, and West had responded briefly but kindly, but Annabel had noticed both Raina and Landon Dunkin never acknowledged that Lucy had said anything about her mother at all. Were the Dunkins trying to be thoughtful of Annabel, thinking that hearing about West's late wife would be uncomfortable for her? Or perhaps it was simply difficult for the Dunkins to talk about the daughter they'd lost. But as dinner wore on, Annabel realized that every time Lucy mentioned her mother, Raina changed the subject.

"I'm looking forward to our girls' day tomorrow after school," Raina said to Lucy. "I love taking you to the library and reading you a story. No matter how big you get, I hope you'll always let me read to you."

Lucy smiled. "What if I'm too big to fit on your lap?"

"Never," Raina said. "Even if you squash me, that's okay."

Lucy laughed so hard that even Raina couldn't stop herself from laughing. "Mommy used to read Winnie the Pooh books to me sometimes before bed." She took a sip of her water. "My favorite character is Eeyore."

"Well, isn't it nice that Annabel can read to you at home now?" Raina said, then cleared her throat.

Lucy looked at Annabel, then down at her plate. Seemed clear to Annabel that Lucy wanted—needed— to talk about her mother but was being shut down.

"I have a surprise for you at home from our wedding trip," West said to Lucy, and the girl brightened. "It might have something to do with Eeyore."

"I love Eeyore!" Lucy said.

"Isn't she getting a little old for that?" Raina said under her breath to West. "She's in first grade now, not preschool."

Annabel glanced at West, and it was clear he was controlling himself before he spoke. But before he could say anything, Mr. Dunkin asked Lucy if she'd like to help him clear the table so they could have dessert faster. Lucy flew out of her chair and carried her plate to the kitchen.

"I'll help too," West said, bolting up and gathering dishes and bringing them into the kitchen.

Interesting, Annabel thought. At first she figured the Dunkins were just very old-fashioned and old school, what with the proper this and that and pink, frilly room. But with Mr. Dunkin having cooked the roast and clearing the table, clearly the Dunkins weren't all that blindly traditional. Something else seemed to be driving Raina Dunkin to be on West's case to the degree she was. And since Annabel had no doubt she'd be spending quite a bit of time with the Dunkins, she was sure she'd find out what it was.

Apple pie and coffee consumed, West collected Lucy's overnight bag, and the three of them walked to the door.

"So I've decided that I'd like us all to have Sunday dinner *every* week," Raina said. "We'll alternate houses. See you at your place next Sunday. Of course, I may drop in a couple of times during the week to see my grandbaby."

West smiled tightly. "Thank you for dinner, Raina, Landon."

Finally they were out the door, Annabel's shoulders relaxing.

"That went well," West whispered as he held open the passenger door of his pickup. "Thank you."

Annabel nodded and got inside the truck. "I think everything's going to be fine from now on."

Lucy kept up her adorable chitchat all the way back to the ranch, how she and her father were building a LEGO donkey house for Eeyore.

West pulled up in front of the ranch house. "Lucy and I do rounds after dinner every night. Want to join us?"

"You can meet the calves," Lucy said to Annabel. "The little brown one is my favorite, but something is wrong with his leg. He's still my very favorite, though."

"Well, I'd love to meet him."

Lucy smiled and Annabel told West she'd take Lucy upstairs to help her change, then would change herself and meet him back downstairs.

"So far, so great," he said. "I'd say this marriage is definitely doing its job," he whispered in her ear.

Lucy's room at her dad's house was a stark contrast to her princess room at her grandparents'. The furniture was all "little girl"—white bed and matching dresser with yellow and blue flowers with a big oval mirror atop it—but the touches, the posters on the walls, the toys, the LEGOs, the robots, the remote-control car and the stuffed beagle collection, that seemed all Lucy. And maybe West. A big poster of a rodeo advertisement took up one wall, and several posters of cartoony animals were all over another. A children's table with a robot, a stuffed Big Bird and a doll on the chairs stood in a corner, a bright orange bean bag beside shelves full of books.

Annabel moved to the closet and slid open the white

door. "Wow, you have a lot of clothes," she said, trying to move hangers aside so that Lucy could get to her tops and bottoms more easily.

"I have a favorites drawer in my dresser," Lucy said. "I never go into my closet unless Nana wants to pick out an outfit for me."

"What's in your favorites drawer?" Annabel asked.

Lucy walked over to the white dresser and pulled open the bottom drawer. "Way in the back I keep my favorite pants and shirts so Nana won't throw them away. She says they're not little-lady-like." Lucy pulled out a pair of faded green cotton pants with frayed hems and a small hole in the knee. "These are my best climbing pants and my absolute favorites. Do you want to know why?"

Annabel kneeled down. "Yes."

Lucy came closer and moved aside a swath of Annabel's hair and cupped her hand between her mouth and Annabel's ear. "I was wearing them the last time I saw Mommy."

Annabel's heart squeezed. "Oh, Lucy. I can understand why they're so special to you, then."

"Nana says they belong in the trash because they're so raggedy, but Daddy said I don't have to throw them out."

"Your daddy's right. You know what? The last time I saw my mom, she made me breakfast before school—sourdough toast with apple butter. And then she and my dad got into a car accident and I never saw them again. So anytime I miss my mom, I make myself some sourdough toast with apple butter, and I feel her with me."

"That's how I feel when I wear my green pants,"

Lucy said. "That's my mama," she added, pointing at a photograph on top of the dresser.

Annabel stared at a photo of Lorna Dunkin, beautiful Lorna Dunkin, holding Lucy as a baby. Lucy looked so much like her dad, but she had her mother's eye color and the elfin chin.

"You guys coming?" West called from downstairs.

"Coming, Daddy!" Lucy shouted.

Annabel smiled at Lucy. "Guess we'd better head down. Want to wear your green pants?"

"I want to wear my orange pants," Lucy said, taking out a pair of pumpkin-colored leggings. "With this shirt," she added, grabbing a bright pink tank top with a comical sea lion on the front. "My dad bought these for me when he went to a cow sale last week in Austin."

Lucy changed out of her top and skirt and put them in her hamper, then slid on the tank top and leggings and slipped her feet into red sneakers.

"I can understand why these clothes are special to you, since your dad got them for you on a trip. See these earrings?" Annabel titled her head. "My dad bought the same pair for me and my two sisters the last Christmas we had together. I love wearing them."

Lucy nodded and handed Annabel a sparkly hair band. "Will you make me a ponytail?"

Annabel gathered Lucy's beautiful ringlets and in seconds had her hair in a high ponytail. "There."

Lucy stared at Annabel for a long moment. "Oh, I forgot—thank you."

Annabel grinned at her. Nana would be proud. Maybe not of the mismatched clothes, but the little girl was a dear and Annabel realized that Lucy had her heart already, just a few hours into this stepmother business.

What would it be like in a few days? Weeks? Months? There would come a time when West had learned what he needed to satisfy the Dunkins and Annabel would be expected to leave.

As Lucy slid her little hand into hers, Annabel realized she'd better be very careful with how much she let these people—West and Lucy—into her heart. As if she could control it.

When West, Annabel and Lucy got back to the house after a tour of the barn for Annabel, Annabel suggested a cooking lesson for the two of them, and Lucy was so excited that West gave up on the idea of grilling burgers, his go-to dinner. For a minute there, he'd actually forgotten that he didn't have to figure out dinner, he didn't have to fire up the grill for burgers that were either too pink inside or burned. Annabel was here, Annabel was his wife, Annabel would be making dinner, something delicious and healthy.

With Lucy all washed up and standing on her step stool, Annabel announced they were making chicken saltimbocca, which involved spinach, prosciutto and Parmesan, with a side of rosemary roast potatoes. As he cut up the potatoes, following a recipe Annabel gave him, he loved watching Annabel and Lucy interact, his daughter asking if spinach would really make her stronger (yes, per Annabel), what "poshoot" was and how to say it, and how patient and kind Annabel was to the little girl. As he coated the potatoes with seasoning and then got them on a baking sheet, he couldn't help noticing that Lucy seemed to adore her stepmother, hanging on her every word. And Annabel let Lucy do a lot, rolling up the chicken with its stuffing and securing with toothpicks, Lucy's favorite part. West found himself paying attention, watching how Annabel adjusted the heat and kept checking for doneness. But of course he'd forgotten about the potatoes and rushed over to the stove to check on them, sure they'd be burned until Annabel pointed out the timer she'd set when he put them in the oven. They still had ten minutes to go. And when he took out the tray, his roasted rosemary potatoes looked and smelled so delicious he forked one, blew on it to cool it and gobbled it up, earning himself a laugh from his wife and daughter.

His wife.

West looked over at Annabel as she and Lucy were cleaning up the island. She wasn't really his wife, even if she was legally, and he'd do well to remember that. He hadn't thought enough about how close she and Lucy might get. After one day together, his daughter thought Annabel hung the moon. What would their relationship be like after a few months?

Maybe he should call a halt to the bonding, try to keep things a bit more…what? Was he supposed to tell Annabel to be standoffish with his daughter? Of course not. So how could he protect Lucy from having her heart broken when Annabel left?

He felt like a damned fool. The whole point of this was to save his family, keep Lucy with him. Now he was setting her up for a broken heart? Why the hell hadn't he thought this through?

He felt Annabel watching him and turned away. Somehow he'd get through dinner and then he and his *wife* would need to talk about how they were going to save Lucy from themselves.

* * *

With Lucy long asleep, the kitchen spotless and An-nabel zonked, she finally had to head upstairs to bed. Her and West's bed. A little while ago he'd said he was going to the barn to check on the calves again.

When she walked into the bedroom, a rectangular room dominated by a king-size bed with an iron head-board, she noticed something new on the double wooden dresser across from the bed. A photograph that hadn't been there when she woke up that morning.

Their wedding picture. One of the selfies West had taken.

She picked up the silver frame, taking in her smile, which looked so genuine. *You're happy because you're in love*, she knew. *And because you just married the guy, albeit for reasons that had little to do with love.*

Or a lot. If she hadn't loved West, cared deeply about him, she wouldn't have married him, not even to save Hurley's. She would have found another way.

"I thought the wedding photo was necessary," West said as he came into the bedroom. "I printed it out this afternoon. Makes this all seem more real, don't you think?"

"Well, we *are* really married," she pointed out, suddenly feeling...deflated.

He walked over and looked at the photo, then headed to the window and stared out at the inky night. "I know. And as we were saying our good-nights to Lucy, I couldn't stop thinking about how this is going to af-fect her." He turned to face Annabel, his expression grim. "When it's time for you to go, I mean. I'd been so focused on saving my family that I didn't consider how she'd feel about you, what having a stepmother would really mean to *her*." He shook his head. "God, I keep messing up. One mistake after another."

She walked over to him and put her hand on his shoulder. "One thing at a time, West. You had to deal with an immediate threat and you dealt with it."

He stiffened for a moment, and she pulled her hand away, feeling like a fool. Why did she keep touching him when he clearly didn't want her to?

He looked at her, and she thought he was going to say something, but he moved to the bed and dropped down, his head in his hands. "I guess."

Buck up, Annabel. He needs you right now, so forget your knotted-up heart. She sucked in a breath. "No 'I guess,' West. That's exactly what you did and it was necessary. Look, I'm not entirely sure about this, but perhaps we should take steps so that Lucy and I don't get too close. I can be more of a live-in sitter than a—"

"Mother?"

She nodded, her eyes filling with tears. Earlier, when she'd helped Lucy get dressed, she felt like a mother for the first time in her life—and she worried that with her luck in the romance department, she'd never know that feeling. She loved talking to Lucy about her favorite things, about her mother, putting her hair into a ponytail. She loved teaching her to cook, watching Lucy sprinkle the Parmesan cheese onto the slices of prosciutto.

This is all part of motherhood, she'd thought then, as she talked to Lucy about her green pants, as she reminded her to wash up for cooking and again for dinner. As she read Lucy three bedtime stories tonight because she enjoyed it so much, watching the little girl's eyes flutter closed, her heart pinging when West came in and kissed his daughter's forehead.

"I love you, Daddy," Lucy had said, half-asleep, her arm around her beloved Eeyore. "And I love An—"

Lucy had fallen asleep before she could finish the sentence, but the look West had given her wasn't "Aw, isn't that sweet that she loves her new stepmother?"

It was one of trepidation, flat-out fear.

Ah. This was where he was coming from. Now she understood. He was looking out for his daughter and rightly so.

And without knowing it, he was looking out for Annabel too. She was a stand-in, that was all. It wasn't fair to let Lucy get attached to her just as it wasn't fair for her to get attached to Lucy—they would be very hurt when it came time for Annabel to go.

He got up and shoved his hands in his pockets. "Maybe you should keep working at Hurley's so you can't be around as much. I don't know." He paced to the windows, letting his head drop back. "No, that's just as wrong. It's still playing a damned game."

"Then let's just do what feels right," she said. "Always. And sometimes that's only something you can know in the moment." Really, Annabel had no idea what she was doing, but this was the truest thing she knew.

He looked at her, his expression brightening. "Yeah. Let's just do what feels right."

"Which is your side?" she asked, gesturing at the bed.

He pointed. "Closest to the door. I get up before dawn, so that's probably better anyway."

She stared at the bed. "Well, I guess I'll turn in."

"Me too," he said.

She bit her lip and went over to the dresser, where he'd cleared a few drawers for her earlier that afternoon. She pulled out her yoga pants and a T-shirt.

He waited, as though expecting her to strip right then and there. Then he seemed to realize she wanted some privacy. "Oh. Right. I'll, uh, go check on Lucy."

When he came back, she was under the covers on the far side of the big bed. The quilt was soft and comfortable and she pulled it up to her chin.

"Everything okay?"

He nodded, sitting down on the edge of the bed, facing away from her. She could hear him removing his jeans. Then he was lying down on his back, staring up at the ceiling the way she was.

They'd decided to keep things platonic and that was the right thing to do. For both of them. But she couldn't stop thinking about the way he'd undressed her in their hotel room, how he'd taken her hands and stretched them up over her head, how he'd kissed every inch of her. She closed her eyes, remembering, wishing things were different. But how could they be?

West shifted. Then shifted again. Then fluffed his pillow and punched it and refluffed it. Then he was back to staring at the ceiling. Did he want her too? He had on their wedding night. Unless, as he'd told her, half a glass of champagne and the emotion of the day got to him. Plus, a naked woman in his bed and all that.

"Awkward, huh?" he said.

"Just a little."

But then she heard the pitter-patter of four feet and suddenly Daisy was on the bed, finding a spot right between them. She spun around a few times, digging at the quilt with her paws and her nose, then settled like a lump.

West laughed, heartily, and so did she. "Well, good night, then."

"Good night," she whispered, wanting to smile and cry at the same time.

Chapter Nine

When Annabel woke up on Monday morning, she decided to make "let's just do what feels right in the moment" her new motto, since she'd never been responsible for getting a child ready for school before.

Lucy had taken a bubble bath the night before, so when Annabel heard Lucy's alarm clock go off, a song from the movie *Frozen*, she went into Lucy's room to find the little girl already out of bed and serving tea to the robot, stuffed big Bird and her Eeyore. For fifteen minutes they'd played tea, and then Annabel let her know it was time to get dressed.

"What's today again?" Lucy asked. "Monday, right?"

Annabel nodded.

"On Mondays, Nana picks me up from school, so I should probably wear something Nana likes. She gets kind of mad if I'm wearing play clothes."

"Well, why don't you pick something out of your closet, then?" Annabel said, figuring that would be a good compromise.

"This!" Lucy said, putting on an adorable pink and white cotton dress with eyelet trim. It was pretty but not fussy. "Should I wear my pink sneakers to match? Nana likes when I match."

"Sounds good to me," Annabel said.

They headed into the bathroom for Lucy to wash up. Annabel dampened her hands and neatened Lucy's ringlets, giving them a little fluff.

Lucy beamed up at her. "I'm so starving."

"Let's go make some scrambled eggs and toast with a side of fruit salad. Sound good? We'll make some for your dad too."

But when they got into the kitchen, the smell of bacon frying told her that West was already making breakfast. He had the folder of breakfast recipes open on the island, a carton of eggs and the bread and the bacon and butter a jumble with plates and utensils.

"The bacon is done a little too early, since the eggs aren't ready, but hey, I didn't burn the bacon," he said with a smile. He stepped over to give Lucy a kiss on her head. "Thirty more seconds or so," he added, stirring the eggs, "and voilà. Done." He slid the eggs onto a platter and set it down on the table next to the plate of bacon. The toaster oven dinged and a plate of toast followed.

"Wow," Annabel said. "Everything looks really good." Okay, the bacon was actually overdone, as were the eggs, and the toast would be cold by the time he got it buttered and on a plate. But still, for West, this was a great start.

West bowed, making Lucy laugh. He made her a plate, adding some cherries to the side. "I had the best teacher."

"Annabel made my hair look nice," Lucy said, taking a bite of bacon.

"You look lovely," West said, eyeing her outfit. "You remembered you have girls' day with Nana after school. Good job," he added, high-fiving Lucy.

"Annabel's coming too, right?" Lucy said. "She's a girl."

Annabel froze. Oh God no. "Well, I think girls' day is special time for you and your grandmother."

"I guess," Lucy said after a bite of scrambled egg.

"I made your favorite snack for today," West said, pointing to the brown bag on the kitchen counter next to Lucy's backpack. "A mini bagel and cream cheese. And I packed some of these cherries I know you love."

Annabel glanced at him. "I would have done that."

"Well, I have to learn sometime, like you said, right?"

As Lucy smiled around a mouthful of toast, Annabel helped herself to coffee. So far, this was going well. She didn't feel out of place here. Lucy was adorable and made Annabel's first official morning as a stepmother on duty pretty darned easy—as did West. She froze, realizing how easy he had made it; he'd cooked a decent breakfast, even if the timing was a bit off. He'd packed a good snack for Lucy and drawn a smiley face on the bag. If he kept this up, he wouldn't need her anymore. Sure, they'd have to give it a good few months before they could go their separate ways. But it was clear that West wanted to be the father Lucy needed, wanted to cook for her, help her dress, take good care of her. He'd work overtime on that; breakfast was a case in point.

And soon she'd be back at the apricot Victorian.

"Let's get you to the bus stop," West said, glancing at the clock.

"You too, Annabel," Lucy said, taking her hand. "And Daisy. She comes every morning."

They headed out, the beagle sniffing her way ahead of them. Just a short way up the road, the big yellow school bus stopped and Lucy raced on, waving at them from her seat. Annabel waved too, her heart in her throat. On the way back, her cell phone rang—an unfamiliar number.

She shrugged at West.

"Hello?"

"Annabel, it's Raina Dunkin. How are you, dear?"

"Just fine. How are you?" She turned to West. *Raina*, she mouthed, and he raised an eyebrow.

"Every Monday I pick up Lucy from school and we have a girls' day. We stop at the smoothie place, do a little shopping up and down Blue Gulch Street, spend a little time at the library. I'd love for you to join us."

Every Monday? she almost choked out. She thought of Lucy, so hopeful that she'd go, so of course she had to say yes.

"So nice of you to invite me, Raina. I'll meet you both in front of the school."

When she put her phone back in her pocket, West put his arm around her shoulder. "If you survive today, Raina with no buffer—well, other than a six-year-old—you can survive anything."

Even the shattered heart I'm in for? she wondered.

By noon, the last of the calves were fed and West was about to go back to the house to practice his chicken salad when his cell phone rang. Jonathan McNeal. West had met Jonathan at Lucy's grief counseling meetings last year. For a couple of months after Lorna died, West had taken Lucy to the sessions for children; the faces of all those kids who'd lost parents, siblings, grandparents, caretakers were heartbreaking. The sessions had helped Lucy, though. She'd gotten comfort from listening to other kids talk about their loss, and twice she'd spoken up about her mother being in heaven and how every time she wished on a star she wished her mother could come back *even though I know she can't cuz she's in heaven now.* West's eyes would well up and he'd have to blink hard to clear them. More than once, Jonathan McNeal, who'd lost his older son and brought his younger boy to the sessions, had handed him a tissue; West never thought to bring them for himself.

"West, Timmy's been having some issues at school, acting out, and I think it's because his brother's birthday is coming up and it's reminding him of the accident and the loss all over again. I remember you saying that you started some kind of therapeutic pony riding program for Lucy back when her mother died and that it helped. Are you still running that program?"

"Truth be told, I never really had a program. I just did it with Lucy myself at our ranch. But I'd be happy to do the same for Timmy. Twice a week for as long as it takes."

"Can we start right away? How's Wednesday?"

West could hear the desperation in Jonathan's voice. "Wednesday's fine. Right after school. Would it help if Lucy's there on her own pony or do you think Timmy would prefer that it's just him?"

"Oh, I think he'd like having Lucy there, see her doing it and all that."

After they hung up, West went back to the barn. He had four ponies—one, Starlight, was Lucy's—and he always had a few on hand for sale. Back when his brother died, West rode his favorite horse, Donald, who his parents had given to him as a foal when West was seven. West had named him after an old hand of his father's, a wizened man who was always kind to West, teaching him about horses and cattle and how you can tell the weather by the scent of the air, by the wind, by how your knees felt. When the news came of Garrett's death, West had ridden Donald for hours, stopping only to give Donald a break. On one of those breaks, Annabel had found him, crying like a baby on the flat-topped boulder he always used as a destination, somewhere to go when he had nowhere to go, nothing to do. The boulder used to be on town land, but when West's ranch had begun doing well and then really started becoming profitable, he bought more acreage and now that boulder was on his property. He liked that.

Timmy McNeal. He thought of that little blond seven-year-old with his tear-streaked face, his older brother gone in a stupid four-wheeler accident. West kicked himself for not thinking of offering Timmy the structured pony rides; he'd been so focused on Lucy, her howls scaring him so deeply that he didn't know if he was coming or going half the time. She'd scream in the middle of breakfast, while eating a piece of toast, just sit there screaming for her mother. And the pony rides helped. He'd had her pick out her own pony and she'd gone right for a beautiful chestnut Haflinger with a white mane and tail and named her Starlight. Daisy, their beagle, had been a huge source of comfort for Lucy, but something about the whole process—getting atop the small horse, learning to ride, the connection between them, grooming her and caring for her—slowly worked its magic.

West looked over at the four ponies grazing in the side pasture and decided to let Timmy choose his own among the three available. His stomach growled and he went inside the house and straight into the kitchen. The refrigerator was a surprise—so full and organized. *Thank you, Annabel Hurley Montgomery.* He'd never seen anything like it. He was so hungry he scarfed down a banana, then grabbed the folder of lunch recipes from the neat stack on the counter near the cookbooks Annabel had brought over. He flipped through them for chicken salad and smiled at the parenthesis: (Gram Hurley's fifty-year-old secret recipe.) The sooner he learned how to make a decent sandwich, a decent dinner, the way he'd done okay with breakfast that morning, the sooner he could appease the Dunkins and set Annabel free. After all she'd done for him, he owed her that much.

No matter what feeling she stirred in his gut, in his head, in his heart…and other places. She'd done him the favor of all favors, and throwing money at Hurley's could never begin to repay her. She deserved better than him, just as his parents had once said. And he was going to make sure she got better. So even though his appetite wasn't exactly as strong as it had been before he started thinking about Annabel and having to let her go someday, he ripped apart the chicken, which helped, then studied the recipe and got out the ingredients. Stupid chicken salad was Annabel's ticket to a better life, a better man. A different man.

Annabel sat in the office at Hurley's, going over the books, the experience a lot different with commas in the restaurant's bank balance. Just a few days ago, she'd stared at the Excel program her gram had painstakingly learned and had her stomach in knots. Now Annabel was perusing sites for dishware etched with cowboys and cacti, for heavier silverware that felt good in the hand, and collecting names of carpenters for the addition she was thinking about.

Her phone rang and she hoped it was Raina, letting her know she'd changed her mind, that girls' day should be just Nana and grandchild. But it wasn't Raina. Georgia's Houston number flashed on the tiny screen.

Annabel jumped up. "Georgia!"

"Annabel, I'm so sorry I've been out of touch," her older sister said, and relief at hearing Georgia's voice swept through Annabel. "Is Gram all right? Please tell me she's all right."

"Well, she's not a hundred percent and tests were inconclusive. On doctor's orders she's been resting this past week, taking it easy, but she got the go-ahead at this morning's appointment to get back on her feet, take walks, do some light cooking."

Georgia was silent, but Annabel knew her sister was crying and trying very hard not to be heard. "I'm so happy to hear that."

"Georgia, what's keeping you in Houston? Something must be going on. Right?"

"Right. But please don't worry. I'm figuring things out and I'll be home as soon as I can. I promise. Please tell Gram and Clem not to worry. I just need to take care of some things here, okay?"

Annabel trusted Georgia; she was the smartest, most levelheaded person Annabel knew. If Georgia said not to worry, Annabel would try very hard not to. She'd come home when she could.

"It's so good to hear your voice, Annabel. So, so good."

"Yours too, Georgia. I love you."

Her sister was quiet again, and Annabel knew she'd made her cry. "Love you too, Annabel. Bye for now."

When Georgia clicked off, Annabel held the phone against her heart and said a little prayer for her sister, then went to tell her grandmother and Clem that she'd heard from Georgia and that she sounded all right and was wrapping up some personal business she couldn't talk about. Clementine was sure it had to do with a man. Gram said it might be business related, since Georgia was an executive.

And that was when Annabel got either a very good or a very bad idea in her head. She grabbed her purse and headed down Blue Gulch Street to the police station before she could change her mind. The secretary at the front desk called over Detective Nick Slater and one look at the dark-haired, dark-eyed cop with the intense expression, and Annabel figured he'd tell her Georgia was an adult, sorry, nothing he could do. But it turned out that Detective Slater was going to Houston in two weeks for a police academy reunion, and he'd check things out while he was in the city. Since he didn't know Georgia, he asked that Annabel text him a few recent photos of her and addresses of where she lived and worked. Annabel was so grateful she wished she could do something special for the cop, but the best she could do was offer him dinner for two on the house at Hurley's.

She left the police station feeling so much better that she was ready to face Raina Dunkin.

So far, so good. Annabel, Raina and Lucy sat on a colorful padded bench in Sierra's Smoothie Shop, a tiny juice bar near the library, awaiting their drinks. Lucy's kiddie-sized strawberry-banana smoothie was ready first, but when the barista called it out, Raina wagged her finger at Lucy.

"A little lady with nice manners waits for everyone's drinks to be ready," Raina told her.

"Okay, Nana," Lucy said, her big hazel eyes on the pink-red smoothie on the counter.

Finally two larger smoothies appeared on the counter. Annabel also ordered strawberry-banana and Raina chose mixed berry.

"Now, Nana?" Lucy asked, and at her grandmother's nod she hurried over and picked up her drink with two hands, took a sip and then headed over to the far side of the shop where a giant abacus with brightly colored beads stood in the corner.

Raina took a sip of her drink. "Ah, isn't that refreshing?" She took another sip, leaving her red lipstick on the straw. "A few weeks ago Landon and I passed by this shop and Lucy and West were in here, so we stopped to say hello. Do you believe West let Lucy order the chocolate-coconut? All sugar. No wonder she runs around like a crazy little boy."

Annabel hoped she hadn't rolled her eyes, which had

been her immediate response. "Well, I'm a firm believer in all things in moderation."

Raina tucked a swath of her ash-blond hair behind her ear. "I suppose. But if West had ordered a fruit-based smoothie for himself—the way you did—Lucy would have too, as she did today. Instead he ordered chocolate, so of course she wanted it. He's always making poor choices like that."

"From what I've seen, West is very committed to Lucy's health. He made a great breakfast this morning—eggs, bacon, whole wheat toast, fruit cup. No chocolate pudding anywhere to be seen."

Raina made her trademark sneer. "That's your influence, Annabel." She patted Annabel's hand, her gaze on the diamond wedding band. "That's a lovely ring. I'm so relieved you married West and will be guiding our little Lucy. I can tell you had a hand in helping Lucy get dressed this morning. I bought that adorable dress for her a few months ago."

Annabel smiled. "Her closet is full of pretty clothes. But I guess West isn't up on little girl fashion the way Lorna had been. I had to explain to him what leggings are."

Instead of responding, Raina turned her attention to Lucy and called out, "Lucy, let's head over to the library and pick out a few books. We can finish our drinks on the way."

Interesting. The woman changed the subject whenever her daughter's name came up. Was talking about Lorna too painful?

At the library, Lucy picked out three books, then sat on her nana's lap, her head leaning against Raina's chest as Raina read, with great feeling, from a picture book about a beagle.

"Beagles are my favorite kind of dog," Lucy said, tapping the two illustrations of the beagle on the page.

Raina kissed the top of Lucy's head. "I know. That's why I wanted to read this book. You're lucky to have such a sweet beagle at home."

"I gave Daisy only one bite of my eggs this morning," Lucy whispered. "I used to feed her a lot more, but Daddy cooks so good now."

Raina winked at Annabel and gave Lucy a kiss on the cheek. "I'm very glad to hear that. Annabel must be a very good cooking teacher."

Lucy shot Annabel a big grin. "Can you read more, Nana?"

Annabel watched grandmother and granddaughter, confused by Raina Dunkin. One minute she was insufferable, putting down West or complaining about a chocolate smoothie, and the next she was being absolutely lovely.

When Raina finished reading, Lucy darted off her lap and raced over to shelves of picture books. "Lucy, little ladies don't conduct themselves that way. Come back here and sit on my lap and slide off properly, then walk to the shelf."

"Yes, Nana," Lucy said, walking back over, climbing onto her grandmother's lap, then gingerly hopping off and walking slowly over to the shelf and pulling out a book.

Back to insufferable in five seconds flat, Annabel thought.

"Raina! How lovely to see you," came a voice Annabel thought she recognized. She glanced over at the woman, similar age to Raina, kissing her on the cheek, a little boy holding a small truck beside her. "Oh, look at darling Lucy. She looks so much like Lorna, doesn't she?"

Raina gave the woman a tight smile, then glanced at Annabel. "We'd better run, Annabel. Lucy, come, dear." She turned to the woman. "So nice to see you. Give my best to Dave." Then she hurried Annabel and Lucy toward the checkout desk, making small talk with the librarian.

Outside, Raina seemed back to herself, chatting with Lucy about school and her teacher. As they were nearing Hurley's, across the street, Lucy called out, "It's your restaurant, Annabel."

Annabel looked over at the apricot Victorian shining in the sun, the new sign so much more welcoming than the peeling one had been. "Tomorrow when I'm cooking at lunchtime, I'm going to bring you and Daddy some of our delicious mac and cheese."

Raina looked shocked. "Surely you're not returning to that hot kitchen. Your place is at the ranch, looking after the house and Lucy."

Annabel knew full well that Raina Dunkin had been a real estate agent for two decades, all during Lorna's childhood, so surely she understood that some mothers and stepmothers chose to work or needed to work. Something else was motivating Raina, underneath all this…prissiness, but Annabel didn't know what and couldn't put her finger on what was poking at her.

"I'm going to be working at Hurley's part-time at lunch to keep my hand in," Annabel explained. "And taking on more of a managerial role."

Raina lifted her chin. "As long as it doesn't interfere with caring for Lucy."

Annabel had to remember that she'd married West to save his family. Arguing with Raina over staying home or working full-time or part-time wasn't appropriate. Her marriage wasn't real. So her conversations with Raina should follow suit.

Wait a minute. That was absolutely unacceptable. She wasn't going to pretend to be something she wasn't. She was married to West—that wasn't a lie. She would be herself, holding her tongue if it didn't really make a difference. But now *was* a time to hold her tongue.

"Mrs. Dunkin! How nice to see you!"

That was a voice Annabel would never forget. A high-pitched drawl that used to mock Annabel back in high school. Francie Heff, who'd been one of Lorna's best friends. Annabel hadn't even noticed that they'd stopped right in front of the storefront where Clyde Heff would be opening his Burgertopia and stealing business from Hurley's.

Francie's gaze went right to Annabel's ring. "So it's not just some crazy rumor. You really are married to West Montgomery!" She tapped Lucy's nose as some sort of greeting.

"I really am," Annabel said, forcing a smile.

"Annabel is a wonderful stepmama to our sweet Lucy," Raina said, squeezing Lucy into a hug.

Francie looked Annabel up and down with something of a sneer, then turned to Raina. "Well, Mrs. Dunkin, I still expect you and Mr. Dunkin to come eat at my daddy's new burger café. We're going to have a big grand opening on Friday—doors open at four-thirty. I hope you'll both come. Of course, I won't expect you,

Annabel, since our goal is to run Hurley's right out of business." She laughed as though she were making a joke, but she clearly wasn't. She smiled at Lucy, bending her knees, her hands on her hips. "I'll bet you like hamburgers. I'm going to have a special kids' menu. Oh my, you look so much like Lorna. I miss my old friend so much. You poor baby, Lucy. You must miss your mama something fierce. Tell you what. On opening day, you come and I'll make a special burger just for you."

Lucy could barely muster a smile.

"Thank you, Francie," Raina said. "I'm not sure of our schedule, but if we're free of course we'll come. Give my best to your father." Raina held tightly to Lucy's hand and hurried her down the street, Annabel following quickly.

One glance at Lucy and she could see the girl's face crumpling. "I do miss Mommy."

"Now, now," Raina said, patting Lucy's back. "You have Annabel to take good care of you. I can see she adores you."

That was all true and well and good, but it didn't address the fact that Lucy was crying about her mother, and her grandmother was dismissing that.

But Annabel wouldn't. She kneeled down in front of Lucy. "Honey, it's okay to cry and miss your mother. I miss my mother too." She pulled Lucy into a hug.

A few seconds later, Raina said, "Well, it's five, so I'd better head home. Give your nana a big ol' hug, my sweet girl," she said to Lucy. Lucy sniffled and very robotically hugged her grandmother. "I'll see you both on Sunday for dinner—at your house, honey," she added to Lucy.

Then she turned on her heel and headed down Blue Gulch Street, her shoulders stiff, Annabel thought.

There was more to Raina Dunkin than met the ol' eye. That much Annabel knew for sure.

Chapter Ten

After playing tea party with Lucy and her Eeyore collection, West went down into the kitchen to find Annabel. From the look on her face when she'd come in an hour ago from her girls' day with Raina and Lucy, he figured she'd experienced a little bit of his world.

Annabel was standing in front of the sink. He came up behind her and peered over her shoulder. She was scrubbing baking potatoes. He breathed in the scent of her and wanted to lift her silky auburn hair and kiss the back of her neck. She wore jeans and a yellow sleeveless shirt and was barefoot, her toes a bright pink with orange dots, which he assumed was Lucy's doing. He smiled, imagining his little girl's delight in polishing Annabel's nails.

"I'll do that," he said, forcing his attention from the curve of her hips to what she was doing, then taking the scrub brush. He wanted to do all the cooking while he had Annabel here to teach him. "Never knew you were supposed to clean potatoes. I just usually run them under water and toss them in the oven."

Annabel slid over a bit, leaning against the counter. "Well, to be honest, most everything I do in the kitchen is because that's how my mama did it. Then when my grandmother took me in, I learned her ways also. Now I have a mishmash."

"Speaking of grandmothers, how did today go?"

Annabel poured herself a cup of coffee, added cream and sugar and then slumped down on a chair at the table, which told him the day hadn't been all smoothies and shopping. "A little bit exhausting."

West laughed. "No doubt."

Annabel sat up straight. "West, why doesn't Raina like to talk about Lorna? I noticed she clams up or changes the subject whenever her daughter comes up in conversation. And today, Lucy said she missed her mother and Raina, well, she didn't really address what Lucy said but tried to comfort her with 'well, you have Annabel now.'"

He mentally shook his head. *That woman...* "I've witnessed that myself many times over the past year." He put down the scrub brush and pricked the potatoes the way Annabel had shown him the other day, then was about to carry the plate over to the oven when he remembered to rub them with a little olive oil and season them with some salt and pepper. He was slowly getting the hang of this cooking thing.

A minute later, the potatoes were baking, his oily hands were washed and he sat across from Annabel with his own coffee.

"Have you ever talked to Raina about it?" Annabel asked.

Ha. The last time he did Raina's head practically exploded she'd gotten so angry at him. "I've tried. But you know Raina. And the relationship between her and Lorna was complicated."

Annabel sipped her coffee. "They didn't get along?"

"They had their good days, but things were mostly strained between them. Lorna had once said she couldn't remember a time when they saw eye-to-eye, even when she was a kid. Raina was a Miss Texas runner-up and all about poise and appearances, and Lorna was a wild child. She liked heavy makeup and skimpy clothes and flaunting her body, and Raina hated that. Lorna told me her mother actually paid her to tone down the makeup and dress respectably for school, five dollars a day, and then she'd get to school and put on her makeup and change into her tight shirt and miniskirt and heels in the bathroom before the first bell. And Raina's a big believer in education taking a person places, but Lorna wanted to drop out at sixteen and try her hand at modeling. Raina and Landon paid her to stay in high school."

"Wow," Annabel said. "I'm all for being who you are, but I can definitely understand the Dunkins' side there."

"Oh, it gets worse," West said, topping off his coffee. "Then I came along. I guess I don't need to point out that I wasn't what they had in mind for a son-in-law. When Lorna told her parents she was pregnant, that I was the father, I was living in hand quarters on the Piedmonts' ranch, making close to nothing."

"How did you two meet?"

"She was a year behind me in school, like you, but I'd seen her around the halls and in town. We first met when her friend, Francie, I think her name is, dared Raina to walk up to me my senior year and put her hand on a certain part of my anatomy. Over my jeans, I mean."

"Classy," Annabel said, grimacing.

He laughed. "That was Lorna and her little posse in those days. And Lorna took the dare. I have to say, I was pretty surprised. She did it right in the middle of the hallway. She told me there was more where that came from, but I wasn't interested in Lorna back then."

Annabel's eyebrows rose. "Really? She was a knock-out."

"I guess, but you can't pick what attracts you, you know? Back in high school I had my eye on my science lab partner, a girl named Lorraine. She had a mathlete boyfriend and they went off to Harvard together, but I had a big crush on her."

Annabel laughed. "I remember Lorraine Haskell. She was valedictorian of your class. She wore glasses and dressed in pantsuits every day." The smile faded. "So you're telling me that Lorraine in her glasses and pant-suits was your type and sexy Lorna Dunkin wasn't?"

"That's right." It was true.

Annabel nodded slowly and he had no idea what was going on in that mind of hers, but to be honest, he didn't want to talk about Lorna or the old days. He'd made mistakes then, mistakes that had both terrific and terrible consequences, and he didn't want to get into all that. And he didn't want to be reminded of what his parents had said about him and Annabel. His folks were probably looking down on him right now, shak-ing their heads at the predicament he was in, what he'd dragged Annabel into.

"I'd better get the pork chops going," he said, standing up, a sudden cold deep in his bones.

She was looking at him as though trying to figure out what was going on in *his* mind, but he really just wanted to be alone right now to shake off the past and focus on the now, which involved getting good enough at cooking to impress Raina Dunkin on Sunday.

"I'd be happy to help," she said. "I know you've been up and working the ranch since before sunrise."

"Thanks, but I've got it. I want to make Sunday dinner for the Dunkins. So I need all the practice I can get."

She nodded and slipped out of the kitchen, and part of him wanted to run after her and hold her close and tell her he had no idea what the hell he was doing, that he was trying blind, and he was so damned relieved she was here, helping him, guiding him. But the need in him bothered him and he tamped it down, getting the meat from the refrigerator and setting it on the counter, no idea what to do with it.

He went over to the folders of recipes, pulled out the one marked Dinner and flipped through the pages until he found Gram's Famous Barbecue Pork Chops, determined not to screw up the sauce the way he did the last time he attempted it.

It occurred to him when he was sautéing the onions, butter and garlic in a saucepan that he and Annabel never did finish talking about Raina's habit of shutting down Lucy when his daughter talked about her mother. He'd pointed it out to Raina once and she'd snapped at him to mind his own business, as though his daughter's heart wasn't his business. She'd bitten his head off when he'd pointed *that* out too. So he'd just made a point to override Raina when she'd try to change the subject if Lucy needed to talk about her mother.

One by one he added the rest of the ingredients for the sauce, pretty sure that chili powder and ancho were the same thing, and wondering if his wife, who spoke her mind, God bless her, would soon find herself butting heads with Raina Dunkin.

He really wasn't sure who'd win.

The sight of the apricot Victorian made Annabel's heart skip a beat on Wednesday morning. She'd missed Hurley's so much. She'd worked the lunch shift yesterday, grateful that Martha was back and that she and Hattie and Harold got along so well. Plus, once the lunch rush had stopped, she'd gone into the office and taken care of the business end, going over inventory and bills, and she'd also hired two more waitresses to take some of the pressure off Clementine, who was so good at her job and knew the menu inside and out that she was like three waitresses.

Being back here, even just for a few hours every day, was like a balm. The last two nights she'd tossed and turned to the point that West had turned on the light and asked if she was having a nightmare.

She sort of had been. Maybe it was dumb, but she couldn't get West and his schoolboy crush on Lorraine Haskell out of her mind. Annabel had looked up to the smart, focused older girl, with her bookish ways and scrawny figure, who always seemed so confident. Lorraine Haskell never wore a stitch of makeup and her chest had been even flatter than Annabel's as a sophomore. So if that was West's type, then why had he thrown her over for sexpot Lorna, who went around grabbing guys in the privates?

That night, seven years ago in his barn, when he'd talked so openly, his heart broken, his soul battered, about the loss of his brother and how devastated he was, how alone he was, she'd known that the boy she'd been secretly in love with for years was everything she imagined he was. Annabel was a moment away from ripping off her own jeans and letting him take her virginity, and then West had thrown cold water on them both and they'd left the barn. She remembered seeing his parents outside, noted that they'd all but ignored him. The next day after school, she'd expected to find him waiting for her on "their" rock, but she'd been in for quite a surprise. He'd been on that rock with Lorna, the two of them passionately making out, his hand up her sweater, her hand in the same place she liked to grab in hallways.

He'd never sought Annabel out and she rarely saw him around town except once or twice with Lorna's arm around his waist, her hand in his back pocket.

Why, then? Why would he ignore the girl who was his supposed type, one he'd just spent an amazing, emotional, sensual experience with, for a girl he'd supposedly not been interested in? What could possibly have happened between Annabel leaving that night and the next day after school? It made no sense.

And instead of just asking him, she tossed and she turned and fretted and wondered and came up with nothing.

Uh, West, why did you take up with Lorna the day after you were with me—especially considering you liked the scrawny, bookish type?

Maybe she was afraid of the answer. That it wasn't about type. It wasn't about checklists. It was about chemistry. It was about The Person. And Annabel just hadn't been That Person for West. She wasn't Lorraine Haskell and she wasn't Lorna Dunkin.

He just wasn't that into you. And he still isn't.

A shiver ran up Annabel's spine that had nothing to do with the April breeze coming through the open window of the small office. She closed the window, grimacing at her great view of Clyde's Burgertopia and the bright red sign announcing Grand Opening—Friday! Free Side of Hand-cut Fries or a Loaded Baked Potato with Every Burger!

The baked potato reminded her of Monday night's dinner at the ranch. West had undercooked the pork chops because he'd been afraid of burning them, but his barbecue sauce—Gram's fifty-year-old recipe—was spectacular, and the baked potatoes had been crackly on the outside and soft on the inside. She'd never been so glad for undercooked pork chops in her life because it meant he still needed cooking lessons—still needed her. The pork chops had gone back under the broiler, but West had been elated about his sauce and the potatoes, and when the pork chops were ready they were perfection.

Last night, though, was another story. While Annabel was giving Lucy a fun spa bath, West had been making Cajun chicken po'boys, but one of his ranch hands had called to say a calf had escaped the pen, and by the time West returned to the grill on the back deck, Annabel had gotten Lucy out of the bath because of the smell of smoke rising to the second-floor window, and they'd found the cutlets burned beyond recognition.

"I'll bet Daisy will eat them," Lucy had said, but Daisy gave the air a sniff and padded away.

The look of disappointment—in himself—on West's face had been heartbreaking, and he insisted on trying again. Second time, success. But the incident had bothered West; Annabel had been able to tell that all through dinner as West politely listened to Lucy and chatted with her about this and that, but Annabel could see he was distracted. She'd tried to talk to him about it last night, let him know that these things happened and between taking care of a family, a new wife—especially given their cough-cough *arrangement*—and calving season, he had his hands full. Besides, she'd been there and if the grill had caught on fire, she could have dealt with it.

What if the Dunkins had been over when it happened? he'd said, shaking his head, his expression grim. *They would have said I shouldn't have left the grill unattended. That Lucy could have come out here to play and burned herself. Damn it, I'm her father and I can't be trusted with her. They're right.*

She'd tried to tell him they weren't right, that all parents made mistakes, that the Dunkins had likely made their share. But he'd stomped around between the barn and the house that night after Lucy went to bed.

And then it had been his turn to flip around in bed, and the only thing that had stopped it was when she'd put a hand on his back, meaning to calm him, and he'd gone still and hadn't moved again.

She'd sighed to herself, her eyes welling, and she'd been so exhausted she'd fallen asleep.

Was this what people meant when they said marriage was hard work? Surely not in the first week. Then again, the Montgomerys of Blue Gulch were hardly your typical newlyweds.

Annabel's phone pinged with a text. From her gram. Annabel smiled. Clementine had taught Gram to text when she got sick and it had taken a few days, but Gram had gotten the hang of it.

Miss my girl. Come have tea with me? Love, Gram.

PS—Sneak me in something sweet, will you?

PS—It's Gram again.

Just what the doctor ordered…for both of them.

At least when it came to horses and cattle and land, West didn't mess up. As he saw Jonathan McNeal's blue pickup coming up the drive, he glanced at the range, watching the cattle graze. One of his workers was carrying bales of hay from the trailer and stacking them, the other one cleaning the stables.

Jonathan's pickup came to a stop, and Daisy ran over to greet the visitors.

West waved as he headed over, smiling at the tow-headed little boy who hopped out of the truck. "Hey, Timmy. Glad to see you. Daisy sure likes you," he added, watching the beagle sniff the boy's legs.

The boy didn't smile, didn't say anything, just watched Daisy sniff and look up at him, waiting for a pat. West waited to see if Daisy's magic would work on Timmy—if he'd be able to resist how darned adorable she was—and indeed, Timmy did resist. Which meant West had his work cut out for him. Timmy was hurting. On the phone the other day, West had let Jonathan know that Timmy should be allowed to be 100 percent himself here—no need for his father to "admonish" him for not being polite or any of that jazz. This experience would be for Timmy to be himself, feel everything he was feeling and let it out, no matter what. West could see Jonathan standing back, letting West lead.

West waved at Annabel and Lucy in the pony pasture; Lucy was already atop Starlight, Annabel walking beside them as they walked the perimeter. Timmy stopped and watched—a good sign.

"You like ponies, Timmy?" West asked.

"I guess," was all the boy said.

West led the way to the stables, to where the three ponies stood. Timmy followed, shoulders slumped, but he was looking around—another good sign that he was interested and engaged, that the ponies and the land and riding would be more powerful than the gray cloud of sadness and worry over Timmy's head. The point was to poke holes in that cloud—if not make it go away altogether.

"Timmy, which pony would you like to ride? If you don't have a favorite, you can try another next time you come. And if you do pick a favorite, that pony can always be yours when you come."

Timmy glanced at the horses, then at his feet. "I like the brown one the best."

West smiled. "I like him too. His name is Captain Petey." After a brief introduction to ponies and how to get up on his back, Timmy was in the saddle, his feet in the stirrups. West led him to the pasture where Lucy was waiting.

"I love Captain Petey!" Lucy called over.

Timmy glanced at her. "I like his spots."

"Like your freckles," Lucy said, pointing at his face.

West held his breath, but Timmy touched his face and looked at down Captain Petey, his brown and white markings. "Yeah," he said, his voice brightening. "Like my freckles."

West glanced at Timmy's dad, who looked so relieved that tears shone in his eyes. As Annabel and Lucy walked ahead, West held on to the reins and led, Timmy holding the horn tightly.

"My mama didn't like horses, do you believe that?" Lucy said from up ahead. "I love horses. Different something and something, my mommy used to say."

"Different strokes for different folks," West said, remembering how Lorna used to say that all the time about just about everything.

"Michael, that's my brother, was scared of horses, but I'm not," Timmy said suddenly. "Do you think he sees that Captain Petey is nice?"

"Definitely," West said."

"Can Captain Petey go superfast?" Timmy asked.

"He can, but while you're learning we'll take it slow. Then next time you come you can take him for a trot—that's like a quicker walk."

"If he'll even be here," Timmy said, and burst into tears.

Timmy's dad hurried over and rubbed Timmy's back. "You want to come off, son?"

Timmy shook his head.

"Captain Petey will be here," West assured Timmy. "He stays in the barn and the pasture, so not much can hurt him. And we make sure he's healthy. Yeah, sometimes things can happen you can't control, that's a part of life, but Petey is kept pretty safe."

Timmy was still crying, but he was calming down. "I want to come off so I can pet him. Is that okay?"

"You bet," West said.

For the next half hour, the bunch of them stayed in the pasture, Timmy petting Captain Petey and Starlight, laughing as he and Lucy fed them carrots, Lucy talking a mile a minute about how much she loved Starlight.

And then it was time for the McNeals to go.

"I can't wait to come back and see you," Timmy told Captain Petey, wrapping his arms around the pony.

Captain Petey turned his head and eyed Timmy, which got a big laugh from the boy.

Jonathan mouthed a thank-you at West and they walked over to their pickup.

"This would have been great for me and my sisters when we lost our parents," Annabel said, patting Captain Petey. "We didn't have much exposure to horses and riding, but I can see how it would have helped."

"My brother wanted to start a therapeutic riding program for troubled kids," West said, remembering how Garrett used to talk about the way horses and riding and the freedom of open land could reach kids whose stubbornness ran deep, like West's. "His dream was to be a cop in Austin and start a program for youth. But he never had the chance to make it happen."

"You could start one here in his memory," Annabel said. "A program for grieving children, for troubled youth. You could do so much good, West. It's clear this is your bailiwick."

Huh. Maybe he could start that program. He knew how riding a horse, caring for a horse, could take your mind off your troubles, how trusting a horse could help you open up, the way learning new skills, whether grooming or riding or mucking out a barn, could rebuild confidence. Then again, part of him didn't feel right about going after something that had been so important to his brother. He could imagine his folks thinking he'd screw it up, not do his brother justice.

You know, a lot of what you think your parents think about you might be in your head, Annabel had said the night of his brother's memorial when they were talking in the barn, when she somehow got him to open up. *You see yourself as the troublemaker you used to be, not as the man you're becoming, the man you are.*

He'd wanted to believe that, he really had. But then later that night, he'd come upon them talking about him ruining Annabel's life and there was no doubt what his parents had thought of him. He'd only been home that night because of the memorial, thinking he should stay for a few days, not even sure he was welcome. But after that first night he'd gone back to the Piedmonts' big spread where he had room and board in exchange for being a hand. He'd been directionless then but liked working on a big ranch, a dream just sprouting about having his own place someday, not that he figured he ever would. The day after he'd heard his parents say— in so many words—they hoped Annabel would leave town and live her dream instead of sticking around Blue Gulch for a nobody like him, he figured he'd never amount to much. He'd spotted Lorna Dunkin in the coffee place and she'd offered her sympathy and whispered some sweet nothings in his ear and that was that. She'd helped him forget. About his losses, his brother, his parents' love, Annabel. For about an hour, he had forgotten everything.

He glanced at the range, at the herd, at the land as far as he could see, then at the house and the red barn behind it. The place might have started out as his parents', but he'd turned it from a small farm to one of the most reputable and profitable ranches in town. He'd done good here.

But the therapeutic riding program was his brother's baby and now his brother was gone.

"I'd love to be a part of it," Annabel said. "I could definitely help with the kids who've lost loved ones. Been there, done that." She glanced at him, then quickly whispered, "I mean, even when it's time for me to go, I could come back to work in the program."

The thought of Annabel leaving his house, leaving Lucy, leaving him, tore up his gut. He liked having her here. So did Lucy. Even if every night he had to pretend his hands were tied behind his back so he wouldn't touch her.

He didn't want to talk about her leaving, so he just nodded and said he'd better go help his ranch hands with the hay bales. He kissed Lucy on the head and told her she'd been a good friend to Timmy today, then walked away, wanting to stay with them more than anything right then.

Chapter Eleven

For the rest of the week, after putting Lucy to bed, West spent what little spare time he had in the kitchen. He might not love cooking, but he was getting better at it. Part of him wanted to stay as far away from the kitchen as possible, to be the same old awful cook he'd always been so that Annabel would have to stay and teach him…maybe for years. But he owed it to her to set her free, and he owed it to Lucy to be the father she deserved, which meant practicing his roasts and his pastas.

On Wednesday, close to midnight, he was probably too tired to be trying to figure out what the hell a roux was and he ended up dumping a pound of flour on the floor, which of course Daisy stepped in and tracked all through the living room.

On Thursday, at 2:00 a.m., between a calves' check and wanting to avoid slipping back into bed where beautiful Annabel was sleeping, he let the fettuccini overboil and inadvertently woke her up. Annabel's nose missed nothing.

"You sure are trying your hardest to learn to cook," she said, her expression one West couldn't read.

On Friday night at eleven, thinking he'd try the fettuccini again, that maybe he'd make it as a side with his chicken parmigiana for the Dunkins, he found Annabel in the kitchen, sitting at the table and drawing boxes. She had at least ten pages spread out of little boxes divided in all different way. Apparently Clyde's Burgertopia's grand opening had been such a success earlier that day that Annabel felt it necessary to add a couple of lunch/dinner take-out items to the menu to lure in folks. She and her grandmother and sister had come up with a "po'boy in a box" special lunch to eat in or out with two sides, all in an easy-to-carry-and-eat-from unleakable box in Hurley's trademark apricot color. It was a good reminder that she was very involved in Hurley's success, that she'd married him to keep Hurley's going, that she wanted to be able to get back to her own life as soon as possible. He mentally kicked himself for not thinking of inviting her family over for dinner, showing them the ranch and the house, making them feel welcome to come out anytime. But Annabel was so furiously working on her box design, pouring yet another cup of coffee, that he figured he'd bring it up the next day over breakfast.

On Saturday, he was the first one up, as usual, and after his chores on the ranch, he found Annabel and Lucy making smiley face pancakes with banana slices for eyes, a strawberry for the nose, and a line of blue-

berries for a mouth. Lucy wanted to add hair, so Annabel added a little whipped cream at the top.

"I won't tell Nana," Lucy said, putting a finger to
her lips. "Nana says whipped cream is bad for you."

He caught the look on Annabel's face—which he'd
translate as *oh,* does *she?*

Then Annabel added even a bit more whipped cream
to make longer hair. She turned to Lucy. "Well, I don't
really like keeping secrets. And I try not to do anything
that I wouldn't want the people I love to know about. So
it's perfectly fine for you to tell Nana that I put whipped
cream on your pancakes."

"I think secrets can be fun," Lucy said, and
launched into a story about how her friend Olivia told
her a secret—that Olivia liked the color orange—and
Lucy has never told anyone else. Then she slapped a
hand over her mouth and said, "Oops!"

Annabel and West laughed and promised not to tell.

That night, after Lucy was in bed and West had per-
fected his fettuccini, salting the big pot of water with
a flourish as if he were Jacques Pepin or something,
he went in search of Annabel, who'd been scarce since
she sang Lucy two lullabies and Lucy's eyelids drifted
closed. He went room by room in the house, then the
back deck, where he knew she liked to curl up and read
at night. No Annabel. As he was passing a side window,
he saw a light on in the barn, on the second level. Was
Annabel up there?

He checked on Lucy, made sure she was fast asleep,
then headed out to the barn, the midnight breeze refreshing against his face. The wooden steps leading
up to the loft were right by the front door and he took
them two at a time.

Annabel sat with her knees curled up in the hay, the blanket around her shoulders.

Uh-oh. "You okay?" he asked, staying at the landing.

"Not really." She didn't look at him, instead resting her face on her arm.

He moved closer and sat down next to her, cross-legged, a memory of the two of them up here seven years ago flitting into his mind, of Annabel handing him the thermos of chili, even taking a spoon and a napkin from her pocket. He could still remember how good that chili was, so good that it really had distracted him from grief for the three minutes it took him to devour it. Later he'd been surprised he had an appetite at all.

"What's bothering you?" he asked, pulling his knees up and wrapping his arms around them as she was doing.

She lifted her head. "I hate what I said to Lucy this morning. It's been killing me all day."

"What are you talking about?" Oh God, she was crying. He saw the tears slipping down her cheeks and wanted to pull her into his arms, but he settled for taking her hand and clasping it in both of his. "Annabel, what?"

"I told your six-year-old daughter that I don't like keeping secrets. That I try not to do anything I wouldn't want the people I love to know about." She looked at West, a combination of sadness and anger in her dark brown eyes. "I *am* keeping secrets, West. I did do something I don't want the people I love to know I did." The tears came fast and furious then, and he pulled her against him.

"Annabel, are you talking about us—our marriage?"

She barely managed a nod. "I didn't tell my family

about our arrangement. I let my grandmother and my sister—two people in the world I'm closest to, who I'd do anything for—think that we married for love, that everything is hunky-dory, that my new husband is so generous he stocked Hurley's bank account, that we're newlyweds so busy cocooning together that we haven't come up for air to even invite them over. And do you know *why* I haven't invited them over to the ranch?"

"Actually I was thinking about that last night," he said, his stomach twisting at what she was saying. "Let's have them over Monday night, then. Hurley's is closed Mondays, so Clementine won't be working."

"That's the thing. I don't *want* them to come here. I don't want to drag them any deeper into a lie, West." The tears came again.

"Annabel, we *are* married. That's not a lie."

She was burning to say something, he could see it. But whatever it was would tear him up and he couldn't deal with that, so he grabbed her and kissed her, his hands moving to her face, the back of her head, down to her breasts, where he lingered on their fullness against the thin material of her T-shirt, the strain against his jeans almost unbearable.

"No, West," she said, pushing him off her. "Not again."

He felt his cheeks burn. "Not again? What?"

She bolted up, anger flaming her own cheeks. "Seven years ago. Then our wedding night. Seven years ago you dumped me for Lorna. Then the morning after our wedding, you said that our wedding night was a mistake, that we should be platonic, that our marriage had a job to do. Sex complicates, remember?" Her brown eyes were flashing. "I don't like secrets, West. And I don't like lies. So let's just keep the truth the truth. This marriage is a business arrangement."

"Got it," he gritted out. Damn it. There was so much to say and it was all jumbled in his head. Part of him didn't even know how he felt about half of it. Their marriage did have its damned job to do. Sex did complicate. And he didn't like secrets and lies either. *But, but, damned but.*

"Good. Then we're settled." She let out a deep breath and dusted hay off her jeans, then hurried down the steps, the barn door shutting behind her.

"But this wasn't a lie, Annabel," he whispered. "How bad I want you isn't a lie. The way I'm feeling about you isn't a lie."

He fell back on the hay, staring up at the beams. How *did* he feel about Annabel?

He supposed he felt about Annabel the way he felt about the therapeutic riding program—as though she was something he wasn't really supposed to have, that she wasn't supposed to be his.

He punched into the hay with his fist, anger welling up from somewhere deep inside him. He closed his eyes, remembering how he and Garrett used to wrestle up here, how Garrett would sometimes let him win, though he never let on at the time. Garrett had always been doing stuff like that, quiet little benevolences that had had huge impact. And what had West been doing? Hanging around, getting into trouble, barely graduating from high school because his grades were so bad from skipping school.

Times like this, when he was torn up about himself, he'd let himself think about Lucy, his beautiful little girl, her dark ringlets poking up in every direction, her green pants, her wide smile missing a couple of baby teeth, her questions and her laughter. And he'd know, heart, mind and soul, that he'd done something right, that he was doing something right.

Keeping things platonic with Annabel would let him keep doing that something right. He let out a deep breath, relief flooding him. *Business arrangement*, he said to himself, then repeated it a few times to get it back in his head. *This is just a business arrangement*.

He wouldn't touch Annabel again.

At four o'clock the next day, Sunday, aka Dinner with Dunkins Day, Annabel came down from playing with Lucy in her room to see if West needed help with dinner. He'd insisted on making everything himself. She'd tried to tell him that the Dunkins couldn't possibly expect him to be a great cook after just one week and two days of marriage to a chef, but he'd said, "I got this, thanks," in a tone that told her to beat it.

Fine. Have it your way, she thought.

Except two minutes of pacing later, she'd come back to the kitchen and said, "Let me at least check on things for you."

He trained those driftwood-brown eyes on her. "I said, I've got this."

She'd left the kitchen again, pacing the living room, worrying that he'd undercooked or overcooked the pasta, that he'd added too much garlic to the sauce, that the chicken would be too tough.

Then again, West wasn't the most confident of cooks. If he said he was okay, especially given how important this dinner was, then everything must be all right. And anyway, if his cooking was a big disaster, the Dunkins would just say that thank heavens Annabel was here and that West should stick to ranching from now on.

The doorbell rang at exactly six. West came out to greet Raina and Landon, and they ignored him, fussing over Lucy in her lovely yellow dress, her hair in a high ponytail with a matching yellow hair tie. Raina scooped Lucy up in her arms, then set her down. Landon settled himself in an overstuffed chair and picked up a coffee table book on wild horses, flipping through it.

"That is a lovely dress," Raina said, beaming at Lucy. "What a pretty yellow!"

"Yellow was Mommy's favorite color," Lucy said, twirling around.

Raina smiled at Lucy, then turned to Annabel. "I smell something wonderful! I can't wait to sit down to a home-cooked meal cooked by a talented Dallas chef."

She'd done it again—ignored Lucy saying something about her mother. "Actually, Raina, West did the cooking tonight. I think he wanted you to see how far he's come in the kitchen."

Raina's face fell. "Oh. Well, I'm sure he's picked up something by having a Michelin-starred wife."

Annabel was about to explain how Michelin stars worked, but Raina interrupted her, the older woman's gaze stern on Lucy.

"Lucy," Raina said, "little ladies don't flip their dress hems up and down."

Lucy scrunched up her face in anger and flipped her dress up and down again, then again.

"Lucy, honey," Annabel said, "let your dress be."

Lucy looked at Annabel and burst into tears, then ran up the stairs. A door closed.

"Well, I wasn't expecting this," Raina said, raising her chin and crossing her arms over her chest.

"I'll run up and talk to Lucy. Why don't you sit and enjoy your drink? We'll be right down."

As Annabel turned to head up the stairs, she noticed Raina walking into the living room and looking at the photos on the mantel—two of Annabel and West's wedding photos, one of the Dunkins with Lucy. And one of Lucy with her mother. Raina's gaze lingered on the photo before she lifted her chin again and moved away, standing in front of the window, her back to the room.

Tension seeped into Annabel's muscles and she hurried up the stairs. She knocked on Lucy's door.

"Lucy, it's Annabel." She opened the door and found Lucy sitting on her bed, holding her Eeyore.

"What got you so upset, honey?" Annabel asked, sitting on the edge of the bed.

Lucy shrugged, her face still crestfallen.

Maybe Lucy didn't really know, couldn't articulate it, but Annabel knew the girl had likely been internalizing her grandmother's refusal to talk about Lorna, the constant changing of the subject, and she'd reacted.

"Your dress is so pretty," Annabel said, touching the yellow cotton. "I like that yellow was your mommy's favorite color. My mother's favorite was red."

"I used to draw the sun on all my pictures because Mommy liked yellow."

Annabel's heart squeezed. "I used to draw hearts for that same reason."

Lucy smiled and threw her arms around Annabel. "I'm sorry I was flipping up my dress." The backs of Annabel's eyes pricked with tears at how much this little girl had come to mean to her, how much she... yes, loved her.

She gave her a tight hug. "That's okay, sweetheart. Ready to go back downstairs? You have special company."

"I love Nana and Pop-Pop," Lucy said, scooting off her bed.

Annabel smiled. "They love you too. I can see that for sure."

They headed back downstairs just in time for West to come out of the kitchen and announce that dinner was ready and everyone should head into the dining room.

"Sorry I got mad, Nana," Lucy said, flinging herself at her grandmother.

"Aw, that's okay, my sweet girl," Raina said, giving her a hug.

"What did I miss?" West asked, looking from Raina to Lucy to Annabel. Landon was still turning pages in the book. Annabel smiled to herself. It was clear who wore the pants in that duo.

Raina rolled her eyes. "West, West, West, some things never change!"

"Well, I *was* in the kitchen, Raina," he said in his defense, but his tone was light.

Again the chin lifted. She took Lucy's hand. "How about you lead the way to the dining room?"

West scrunched up his face, and Annabel smiled at him, the only light moment between them since last night in the hayloft. Relief crossed his expression, and her shoulders unknotted a bit. But just a bit.

I love you, you jerk, she wanted to yell.

"Annabel, we're waiting for you," Lucy called from the dining room.

Annabel wanted to cry and laugh and the same time. She did love him. She always had loved him, and now she loved him harder and deeper and more than she ever thought it was possible to love a man.

"I'm happy to help get dinner on the table," she said, forcing another smile.

He stood looking at her for another moment, then said, "Go sit. Everything's under control." He headed back in the kitchen and two seconds later she heard a thud and then a muttered expletive.

West appeared in the dining room with a platter, which he set down in the center of the table. His chicken parmigiana looked good. Too good, Annabel thought, happy for him and sad for herself at the same time. She couldn't exactly wish it were undercooked and that everyone got food poisoning, but she hoped it wouldn't be as delicious as it looked.

It was.

Landon took a bite of the chicken, then another. "You did not make this, West Montgomery." Landon rarely said anything, so that was saying something.

"I did," West said. "I followed Annabel's recipe. Family recipe going back a hundred years."

"You didn't help at all?" Raina said to Annabel. "Come on."

"He wouldn't let me near the kitchen. Scout's honor," Annabel added, holding up the hand gesture.

"Daddy, this is really good."

"Thank you, Lucy. There would have been garlic bread, but I dropped it when I was taking it out of the oven."

Raina laughed. "Now, that sounds like the West I

know. But I have to say, the chicken is delicious and so is the pasta. The sauce is excellent."

The relief across West's face lifted Annabel's heart for him, but it meant her days were numbered. With West's cooking not just passing muster but getting raves, and Lucy's closet sorted into play clothes, school clothes and Nana clothes, the special conditioner Annabel bought for her knotty ringlets making her hair easy to comb after her bath, West could pass the Raina Dunkin Fatherhood Test with flying colors.

No Annabel required.

After Annabel and West saw Lucy to the bus stop on Tuesday, West did his usual hat-tipping at Annabel and headed off to talk to his ranch hands, which was what he'd done yesterday, making himself scarce all day. He'd fallen asleep on the couch, fully dressed, and the sight of him there when she'd come down in the morning hurt worse than anything. Their business arrangement was coming to an end. They'd have to keep up appearances for a while so that it didn't seem strange that they were suddenly splitting up, but soon enough he'd want to find a wife he loved.

Her heart hurting so badly, Annabel drove into town and parked in Hurley's lot, the sight of the restaurant so comforting. She needed a cold meat loaf sandwich and a sweet tea pronto.

Someone was tapping on her car window. When Annabel turned and saw it was none other than Francie Heff, she groaned inwardly. Francie wore her Clyde's Burgertopia hot-pink apron, her ice-blue eyes unusually warm. She must be up to something. Annabel got out of her car, instinctively crossing her arms over her chest.

"Guess what!" Francie said. "My daddy came up with the best idea and his cousin, Stanton, editor of the *Blue Gulch Gazette*, agrees and plans to run a huge story about it."

This couldn't be good. "What's that?"

"We are hereby challenging Hurley's Homestyle Kitchen to a cook-off!"

What-now? A cook-off?

"Who makes the better barbecue burger," Francie continued. "The new kid on the block?" She pointed to Clyde's Burgertopia. "Or the stuffy old institution that's been around forever and ever," she said, nodding at the apricot Victorian. "The *Gazette* will post coverage about the cook-off all week to drum up excitement. We can hold it at Hurley's because you've got the bigger kitchen. We'll each make one barbecue burger, and the mayor will choose the winner. Everyone knows how he loves his burgers." She puffed out her cheeks and cupped her hands way out in front of her flat stomach to indicate his girth. "And he's neutral. He goes way back with your gram *and* my dad. We can trust that he'll be fair."

The mayor did go way back with Gram and ate at Hurley's at least twice a week. He was an old family friend, just as he was of the Heffs. But Annabel was a bit afraid the publicity of the cook-off would call more attention to "the new kid on the block" in the first place—and imagine if the Burgertopia won? The "old stuffy institution" would lose even more business.

"We're too busy for this kind of thing, Francie."

"Ha. Figured you'd say that. We'll just run the story that Hurley's was too chicken to come up against us. I mean, we're willing to do it and imagine if we lost—

a brand-new Burgertopia losing a *burger* contest to a plain ol' granny's Homestyle place."

"You seem awfully sure you're going to win, Francie." The woman probably had a bunch of tricks up her sleeve to cheat their way to victory. Clyde Heff might be a straight shooter, but Francie was a sneak.

Francie laughed. "Of course we will. And we'll have the mayor watching over the cooking and the burgers at all times to ensure that there's no cheating. Even a Goody Two-shoes like you've always been will resort to anything to keep your family business from looking stupid. So I won't put anything past you."

If only you knew, Annabel thought, her stomach hurting from the punch it just took. But then again, Annabel wasn't such a Goody Two-shoes. A nice person, sure. But sometimes you really did have to get in the ring.

"I really don't know, Francie. I'll talk to my grandmother, but you know that she's just recently back on her feet after—"

"There's a ten-thousand-dollar prize for the winner," Francie interrupted, shimmying her shoulders. "Cousin Stanton is loaded. And he's figuring we'll win and that money will go to our family. A big prize like that will get folks' attention and they'll be lining up five deep to watch the cook-off and see who wins. Then, when we take the prize, they'll all cross the street—permanently—for a Clydeburger."

Ten thousand dollars.

That would let Annabel give West back his money and take over the running of Hurley's again. They'd have to forgo the addition and the back patio for outdoor dining, but they'd have ten grand in the bank to keep going.

"Let me talk to my grandmother and sister and I'll let you know."

"I need your answer by closing time today," Francie said, and turned on her kitten heel and headed back across the street.

Annabel jogged up the steps and into the house just as Clementine was coming downstairs.

"Have time for coffee in Gram's room? I need to talk to both of you. Francie Heff has some wild idea."

"We're listening to Francie Heff these days?" Clementine said, raising an eyebrow. "The other day she actually had the nerve to stand right in front of Hurley's and lure people across the street to Clyde's. I heard her stop the Clarks as they were coming up the steps, turning up the drawl—'Have you tried a Clydeburger? Two-for-one special just for today.' And they actually turned around and went to Clyde's."

Annabel shook her head. "Well, she has a new publicity idea, but this one might actually benefit us. Let's go make tea for Gram and we'll talk it out."

Ten minutes later, tea and coffee on a tray, Annabel and Clementine walked into their grandmother's room to find Essie Hurley sitting up, her color better than it had been in a week.

"Gram, you're looking great," Clementine said, rushing over to give her a hug. "It's gorgeous out today. Low seventies this morning. After tea, let's go walk around in the garden till it's time for lunch prep." The past few days her gram had been up and about the house, making her own tea under Clementine's watchful eye. But Annabel could see a new vigor about Essie. Thank God.

"I'm feeling better," Gram said. "I felt really good

yesterday and today when I woke up I had more energy. I think I'm bouncing back."

Annabel's eyes pricked with tears and she ran over to hug her grandmother. "I'm so glad. We've been so scared."

"I know," Essie said. "But don't you worry. I'm getting stronger every day. I think in a few weeks I'll even be ready to cook again—maybe not standing for hours like I used to, but for a bit here and there. I can certainly prep in a chair. And just in time too—turns out Martha misses her family and wants to go back to Austin. Tomorrow's her last day."

Annabel's smile faltered, and then she realized this was good timing for her too. She was needed less at the ranch and could work the dinner shift again. Lucy's sweet face came to mind. Annabel wouldn't be able to meet Lucy at the bus. Or work with her on her addition or sight words.

Focus on Hurley's now, she ordered herself. *You knew the deal when you said yes to West.*

Annabel launched into Francie's proposal, leaving nothing out.

"Ten thousand dollars," Gram repeated. "Not too long ago I would have jumped at the chance to win that much money. But I'm not sure we have to play their game now that we're more financially comfortable, thanks to Annabel's very generous husband."

Do not start crying. Do not start crying. Do not start crying.

But the waterworks started and Annabel couldn't stop. And suddenly she was telling her grandmother and Clementine the whole story, starting with the reason for the marriage proposal and ending with how

West didn't need her anymore and she thought it was only fair to give him back the bulk of the money now that they'd both be going back to square one. Annabel left out the part about how much she loved West, how she wished he loved her.

But West didn't love her. She had to face it and move on.

"I need to earn that ten thousand," Annabel said. "Because then I won't feel as though I'm letting down you and Clem by giving West back his money. We'll have some breathing room, not much, but some. I'll see this marriage through till this Sunday night's dinner with the Dunkins, but I can't do this anymore. Living with him and Lucy is breaking my heart. The longer I stay, the more deeply in love with both of them I'll be."

"Oh, honey," Gram said, pulling Annabel against her and wrapping her arms around her. "You won't be letting us down. We'll be fine no matter what."

"So maybe the cook-off *is* a good idea," Clementine said. "Annabel, you know you'll beat Clyde. I've had their barbecue burger—I paid a teenager five bucks to go order four, and Hattie, Martha, Harold and I tried the competition on opening day. It was good, I'll be honest, but not as good as ours. Our sauce just has that something special. And our burger too."

Annabel smiled. "You're as confident as Francie was that *they'll* win."

"Clyde *does* make a danged good burger," Gram said. "And his barbecue sauce is delicious. I've had his barbecue burgers many times over the years at his big Fourth of July parties. But, Annabel, you could cook circles around Clyde Heff."

"I'm hoping *you'll* do the cook-off, Gram," Anna-

bel said. "Hurley's *is* you. And I think people will want
to see Gram Hurley and Clyde Heff in a battle of the
burgers. Plus, they'll see you're back up on your feet.
If you're up to it."

A gleam appeared in Essie Hurley's eyes. "You bet
I'll do it. What do you say nowadays? Bring it off!"

Clementine laughed. "Bring it *on*, Gram."

"Bring it *on*, Burgertopia!" Gram said, waving her
hand around.

Annabel laughed. Gram was back. Hurley's would
be back too. But an ice-cold hollowness settled in her
stomach and she felt her smile fade. She already missed
West and Lucy. She glanced down at her beautiful wedding ring. How was she ever going to bear sliding it up
and off her finger?

Chapter Twelve

Annabel spent the next couple of days between the ranch and Hurley's, being a good stepmother to Lucy and tasting so many barbecue hamburgers—made by the incomparable Essie Hurley—that she'd probably gained a good five pounds. Each burger was better than the next, the sauce richer.

They were going to win, Annabel knew, her heart heavy. Monday morning she'd be back at the Victorian, working at Hurley's full-time. How would she and West tell Lucy that Annabel was leaving? How would that make sense to a little girl who'd already lost her mother? Annabel and West would have to talk that through, do what was right for Lucy.

On Thursday morning, as Annabel waved goodbye to Lucy on the school bus and watched it head down the road, she turned back toward the ranch, chewing over how the heck she could leave without hurting Lucy. How could Annabel walk out on Lucy? How could she stay with West?

Her ringing phone interrupted her. Raina.

"Annabel, I'm hoping you and Lucy can come over today after school for tea and girl talk," Raina said, a brittle edge in her voice. Something was wrong.

"Raina, is everything all right?"

Raina was quiet for a moment, then said, "Yes, of course. Shall I see you both at three-thirty?"

"We'll be there."

Now she had all day to wonder and speculate. At least it would get her mind off leaving.

Something did seem wrong with Raina, Annabel thought, watching her with Lucy in Raina's elegant living room. For no reason that Annabel could discern, the older woman was dressed up even more than usual, in a pale pink pantsuit with a frilly shell and loads of gold jewelry. There just seemed a strain in her expression. Plus Raina had barely let Lucy off her lap since they'd arrived a half hour ago. She hugged her constantly, read a book to her, then French-braided her hair. But when Annabel went into the kitchen to stack the sandwiches on a tray, she could hear the happy chatter between grandmother and granddaughter. Maybe Raina and Landon had had an argument and Raina just needed some time with her granddaughter.

Then why invite Annabel too?

"My mommy put my hair in this braid for picture day in kindergarten," Lucy was saying. "Look, there's the picture of me on the mantel!"

From the kitchen, Annabel heard the little thud of

Lucy's feet hitting the floor and the sound of her running. To the mantel to look at the photograph, Annabel figured. "Nana, can you reach it for me?"

"No, Lucy. The photograph will stay where it is," Raina said, that edge back in her voice. "And I've told you many times—little ladies don't run inside."

"Well, I'm not a little lady, then!" Lucy shouted.

Oh God. Should Annabel intervene? Should she let Raina handle this? What was overstepping?

The next thing Annabel heard was the sound of the little footsteps running again.

"Lucy! Come back here!" Then silence. Then, "Annabel, Lucy ran out the front door!"

Annabel rushed from the kitchen to find the front door wide-open. She and Raina raced outside; Annabel could just make out Lucy racing around the corner toward busy Blue Gulch Street.

"There she is!" They both charged in the direction Lucy went. But when they got to the intersection of Blue Gulch Street, there was no sign of Lucy.

"Oh no," Raina said, her face stricken. "Where is she?"

"We'll find her. She knows this street, knows where her favorite shops are. I'm sure she's in the coffee shop or the library. We'll find her. You take left, I'll take right. Whoever finds her calls the other."

Raina nodded and headed left toward the library; Annabel went right and raced into the coffee shop, checking all the nooks and crannies and the children's corner. No Lucy. She asked passersby if they had seen a little girl with dark curly hair—no. Annabel rushed into a few more possibilities—no sign of Lucy. She turned around and strained to see down the street. Raina was coming out of the smoothie shop, her expression crest-fallen. She waved at Annabel and shook her head.

Where are you, Lucy? she wondered, panic attacking her stomach and her brain.

Raina hurried over. "I've looked everywhere on that end. There's no sign of her. Oh God, what have I done? Why did I make her so upset that she ran away?"

"I think I know where she is!" Annabel said. "She might have gone to Hurley's backyard. There's a swinging bench—it's where I always went when I was upset as a kid. And Lucy knows Hurley's."

Annabel's phone rang. Clementine.

"Did you know that Lucy is by herself in our backyard?" Clementine asked. "She's on the white swing."

Relief flooded through Annabel. "I just realized that's where she might be. Clem, can you check on her, bring some milk or something? Her grandmother and I will be there in five minutes."

Annabel pocketed her phone. "Raina, I love that little girl, so I'm going to overstep my bounds and tell you that I think it hurts Lucy deeply that you shut her down when she brings up her mother."

Annabel waited for the wrath of Raina Dunkin, but instead Raina's eyes filled with tears and she covered her face with her hands. "I just want Lucy to be... the girl I wished Lorna had been. I know that's terrible. I know it's terrible to wish my own daughter had been different. But she was so rough and wild, running around with half her body exposed, sticking her head out of cars, chugging on a bottle of Jack Daniel's. When she got married so young I thought maybe having one man, a husband, would at least settle her down, but she ran around on West. With a baby at home." Raina sucked in a breath.

"Raina, I—" Annabel tried to think of the right words to say, but she was at a huge loss here.

"You want to know the truth about my last conversation with my daughter?" Raina said, her expression numb. "She told me she was leaving for good, that I should look in on Lucy a couple times a week because West was so inept as a father, could barely break an egg or get Lucy dressed properly." She let out a harsh breath. "I told her she was not going anywhere, that she had a child to take care of and you don't leave your child and she'd better grow up. I yelled at her."

"Oh, Raina, any mother would have said exactly that."

"Well, she didn't listen. You know what she said right before she left? She said that love wasn't enough and added an 'obviously.' I thought a long time about what she meant by that. That my own daughter wasn't enough for me, that West and Lucy weren't enough for her. Maybe I did that to her, by being so hard on her. By trying to make her into something she wasn't. Like I'm doing with Lucy." Her head dropped.

Annabel took Raina's hands and held them. "Lucy is a tomboy. A wonderful, darling tomboy. She likes climbing trees and wearing the green pants she wore the last time she saw her mother."

Raina sniffled. "She told me that once. I shut that down hard inside me, didn't want to hear it. I know I need to let Lucy be herself. And I need to let her talk about her mother."

Annabel put her arm over Raina's shoulders. "And you need to forgive yourself—and your daughter."

Raina nodded, calming down. Annabel pulled out a tissue and Raina dabbed under her eyes.

"I know someone else who feels like he needs forgiveness, forgiveness he'll never get because his parents are gone. Maybe over time you can talk to West here and there about your relationship with Lorna, what you wished you could have done differently, what you wouldn't have done differently. I think that'll help."

"I think I could do some healing there," Raina said, brightening. "He's trying so hard, isn't he? And everyone needs a mother, don't they?"

"Yes," Annabel whispered. "Everyone does. And a wonderful grandmother too."

"Lucy might get darned sick of how wonderful I'm going to be," Raina said, a smile spreading over her tearstained face.

"Never," Annabel said. "Let's go see our girl."

Our girl, Annabel thought, her heart splitting in two.

They hurried across the street and around the side of the house. Curled up on the swing was Lucy, Clementine's arm around her as she read her a Winnie the Pooh book from Hurley's children's section.

Clementine finished the story, then said, "Look, Lucy, you have company."

Lucy looked over, her face crumpling.

Raina walked over, her expression kind and compassionate. "Lucy! I was so scared when I couldn't find you."

"I don't want to be a little lady. I just want to be me." She burst into tears, and Raina hugged her against her.

"Sweetheart, I'm sorry. I'm so sorry. I'm not going to tell you to be a little lady anymore. I only want you to be you. And I didn't mean to make you so upset."

"I just wanted to see the picture," Lucy said. "Mommy made my hair so pretty for picture day." She touched the French braid that Raina had made for her just an hour ago.

Tears filled Raina's eyes. "You want to know something, sweetheart? The reason I got so upset about that photograph? It's that my heart was hurting. Because today was your mama's birthday. She would have been twenty-six years old."

"Today?" Lucy repeated, her head tilting.

Raina nodded. "I know you and Daddy talk about your mama a lot. He probably didn't tell you because you're very young and wouldn't really know what to do with the information. And I think he's right. But I wanted to tell you so you'd understand why Nana was feeling especially sad today."

"Would you feel happy if we had a birthday cake for Mommy?" Lucy asked.

"I would like that," Raina said. "Maybe we can do that every year as a way to honor her."

At Lucy's big smile, she added, "Let's go home and bake that cake now."

"Annabel too?" Lucy asked, smiling up at Annabel.

"Annabel too," Raina said.

As they headed back to the house, Lucy between them, a small hand in each of theirs, Annabel knew that Raina Dunkin had just officially welcomed her to the family. A family she wished more than anything could be hers.

That's interesting, West thought, watching Annabel's car come down the road, Raina's Mercedes right behind it. When the cars came to a stop and everyone got out,

Lucy hopped out and rushed over to him, and instead of telling her that little ladies walk calmly, Raina only smiled. At him too.

That was new.

Raina ignored Daisy, who was sniffing at her shoes. At least that was standard. Raina cleared her throat. "I'd like to talk to you if now's a good time."

Uh-oh. What was this about? He glanced at Annabel, and her very pleasant expression and Lucy's giggles as the barn cat batted Daisy's ear told him it couldn't be all bad.

They walked along the road, Raina keeping her hands clasped in front her. Five minutes later, she finally stopped talking and took a deep breath, then started up again.

"I'm very sorry, West. For how I've treated you this past year. For the past seven years. You were nothing but good to Lorna. And you're a good father. You might not have fed and dressed Lucy the way I would have liked the past year, but she's healthy and happy, isn't she? Because of my behavior, my stubbornness, my own issues, I put Lucy in danger today. She ran away to a busy street on my watch."

There'd been so much to take in the past couple of minutes as Raina had spoken that West didn't even know where to start. All he knew was that he appreciated her honesty and her apology.

"Well, those things happen," he said. "And I'm sure they'll keep happening as Lucy grows up. I hear teenagers can be pretty challenging."

Raina smiled and extended her hand. "Shall we start over?"

West took her hand and shook it, then reached over

to hug Raina and she finally softened and hugged him back for a good fifteen seconds.

As they started walking back toward the house, he pointed at the pasture where the four ponies were grazing. "Raina, I'm thinking—no, not thinking. I'm *starting* a therapeutic riding program at the ranch. For children who've lost loved ones and for troubled youth. But I think adults could benefit from the program, as well. And as someone who's lost a child, you'd be a welcome addition to the volunteer staff, if you're interested."

Raina's eyes welled with tears. "I'd like that very much, West. Thank you." She dabbed under her eyes with a tissue. "Well, I'd better get going. Too much emotion gives me a headache. Plus, I'd like to fill Landon in on everything that's happened. I think he'll be very happy."

As he watched Raina say her goodbyes to Lucy and Annabel, then get back in her car and drive up the road, he shook his head in wonder, his shoulders, his heart, lighter than they'd been in years.

With Lucy settled in bed and Annabel taking her own bubble bath after what had to be a very draining afternoon, West finally sat down at the kitchen table with the *Blue Gulch Gazette* and a cup of coffee. He was just flipping pages, waiting for Annabel to come downstairs so he could fill her in on what he and Raina had talked about, though he was sure Annabel knew already, when his hand froze on the page. An entire section was devoted to a cook-off—a barbecue burger—this Saturday night in Hurley's kitchen between Essie Hurley and Clyde Heff. Mayor Hickham would be judging.

There was a ten-thousand-dollar prize.

Why on earth would Annabel and her grandmother get involved in this?

When he heard Annabel come down the stairs, he went into the living room with the paper. Annabel was in a tank top and yoga pants, her long auburn hair wet, a comb in her hand.

"I'm surprised you, Essie and Clementine agreed to this," he said, pointing at the ad. "This publicity stunt sounds like the Heffs, but not the Hurleys. And it's not like Hurley's Homestyle Kitchen needs the ten grand."

Annabel glanced at the paper, then continued combing her hair. She turned away for a moment, then looked at him. "I'll be able to give you back the money you fronted us."

He stared at her as if she had four heads. "Pay me back? Annabel, we made a deal."

She turned toward the window, staring out at the dark night. "Yes, but you don't need me anymore, West. Especially now that you and Raina are at peace. More than peace. You're family now."

"That doesn't mean I'm backing out of my end of the bargain, Annabel."

"Code of the West and all that. I know. Which is why I'm backing out for both of us. You need to move on and find a real wife. I've been torturing myself about how Lucy would be affected by losing me. But I realized that she needs to grow up with parents who love each other. She needs to see what a marriage really is. What love really is. That's what's fair to her."

He shook his head. "It's like seven years ago all over again," he said, his voice numb. "When I have to let you go."

She stared at him. "What?"

He let it all out, how he overheard his parents the night of his brother's memorial, how they'd basically said he'd ruin Annabel's life by keeping her in Blue Gulch and that was why he'd taken up with Lorna, to keep Annabel from ending up with him, to set her free.

Annabel dropped down on the couch, her expression numb. "I had no idea. You started seeing Lorna because you didn't want me to end up with you?"

"My parents thought I was nothing," he said. "In their eyes, the wrong Montgomery brother died."

"No, West. They didn't say that. I'd bet anything they didn't say those words."

"Not those words. But I know that's how they felt. Garrett was their golden child, made them proud, and then there was me, barely graduated from high school, running around with a rough crowd. They knew I'd drag you down, break your heart. They were probably right. So I let you go."

Annabel got up and walked over to him and took his hands. "They didn't see you, West. Sometimes you can live right in the same house with people—people you've known your whole life and you don't see them. Your parents didn't see you, who you were deep inside, they didn't know you. You sacrificed for me, West. You gave up the girl you wanted to save her from yourself—right or wrong. Doesn't that tell you what a good person you were then?"

He took a deep breath and said nothing.

"You know you're a good person, a good father. West, you're even a good husband in a sham marriage."

He ran a hand through his hair and turned away. "So why do I care so damned much?"

"Because it hurts when people you love, especially people who are supposed to love you, don't see who you really are. But I'll tell you something, West Montgomery. Your parents see you now, trust me. Back in high school and the couple years after when you were rebelling against everything, they were too busy being upset to think about what was behind all that rebellion. Now they might not be here on earth, but they're looking down and watching and seeing and they know what you've done here. What you're doing in your brother's memory."

He shrugged, but Annabel had gotten through. The whole situation with his parents was complicated and would probably always sting, but West had paid tribute to them by turning their ranch into something special, paid tribute to his brother by getting the riding program going—and hell, if he could make peace with Raina Dunkin, he could find a way to make peace in his heart with his own folks.

"Make me a new deal," he said. "If you lose the competition, stay a few more months. Let me keep helping Hurley's. If you win, fine, you'll leave after Sunday dinner with the Dunkins. I'll explain to Lucy that you'll still come over twice a week to help with the riding program and to see her."

Annabel nodded. "You'll have to tell her I'll still be in her life, that I'll always be there for her. That just because I won't be living at the ranch doesn't mean I don't love her."

"You'll tell her that. And I'll make sure she knows it. But we'll cross that bridge if we get to it."

Annabel bit her lip. "We're going to win, West."

He looked away. "Yeah, I know."

"You did more than enough for us and the restaurant. Please don't feel you're letting Hurley's down."

He nodded, said he was going to check on Lucy and spend the night on a cot in the barn, since another calf was having some trouble. A part of him thought he should tell her how he felt about her, how he'd always felt about her, but how was that fair? To make her feel worse about wanting to leave? She'd kept her end of the bargain. Now once again, he had to let her go so she could find happiness.

She stared at him for a moment, then nodded and walked away, his heart splitting in two.

West spent the rest of week avoiding Annabel and the way his chest felt tighter and tighter. He spent all his spare time working on the riding program. He even unveiled a sign on the pony pasture: Garrett Montgomery Memorial Therapeutic Riding Program.

This is for you, brother, he said silently up to the sky. *And for you, Mom and Dad. I think you'd be proud of who I've become.*

Sometimes when you loved someone, you had to let them go. Sometimes you did anything it took to keep them. For just a second West wished he was more the boy everyone thought he used to be, who'd do the wrong thing—so that Annabel would have to stay.

Chapter Thirteen

On Saturday night, it seemed the whole town had gathered on the sidewalks and streets—closed off at the mayor's orders—for the duration of the cook-off at Hurley's Homestyle Kitchen. The dining room was packed to capacity, folks standing in every available inch of space, a big crowd on the porch and on the sidewalk in front of Hurley's.

Here goes everything, Annabel thought as she helped Gram tie her apron around her back. The sight of Essie Hurley strong on her feet, looking so healthy and determined, brought a smile to Annabel's face. Annabel wished her older sister were here to see this; Georgia would be thrilled to watch Gram take down the Heffs; soon enough Detective Slater would be going to Houston and could check up on Georgia for Annabel.

"I can't believe how many people are stuffed in the

dining room, the porch and the backyard," Gram said, peering out the window of her bedroom. "Win or lose, we brought the town together for a fun event."

"Those Heffs know how to publicize, that's for sure," Clementine said. "Even my birth mother is here," she added, upping her chin at the dark-haired woman in jeans and cowboy boots standing by herself across the street. "She's prickly and not into much contact, but I like that she's here, even if she's staying across the street."

Talk about complicated, Annabel thought, glancing at Clementine's birth mother. She'd had Clementine when she was sixteen, and though she lived in Blue Gulch, she still kept contact with Clem to a minimum.

"One day I'll know her whole story," Clementine said. "I hope anyway." She moved away from the window and squeezed her grandmother's hand. "Thank God for my mother and father and for you," she added. "I've been blessed. I never want to forget that."

Gram hugged Clementine. "We're all blessed to have one another. Win or lose at this and that, win or lose tonight, we have one another."

"Speaking of losing," Annabel said, "if Clyde somehow manages to best us, West wants me to stay on a few more months, taking care of Lucy and helping to get the therapeutic riding program off the ground so that I'll feel more comfortable keeping some of the money." *Our marriage will still be doing its job, just more so for Hurley's this time*, she thought. "I don't think that's a good idea, but I agreed. Anyway, I know we'll win and win big. No one can beat your barbecue burger, Gram. Not Clyde, not me, not anyone."

Gram pulled Annabel and Clementine into a hug.

"I love you both so much. I love you and Georgia more than anything on this earth."

"I love you too, Gram," Annabel and Clementine said in unison, hugging their sweet grandmother.

They left the room and headed down the hall, folks calling out "Good luck!" every second. West, Lucy and the Dunkins were seated at a table by the front window, Gram's biscuits and apple butter in front of them with a round of sweet tea.

"Good luck, Essie," West said, standing up to give her a hug. "I haven't had a Clydeburger—wouldn't dream of going over to the dark side, but I know your burger is better anyway."

Gram laughed. "Of course you do."

"Good luck, Miss Gram," Lucy said, making Essie chuckle. She turned to Annabel and gestured to her to kneel down, then moved Annabel's hair out of the way and cupped her hand around Annabel's ear. "I'm wearing my Annabel clothes," Lucy said. "Remember? This is the outfit I wore the first day you were my stepmother."

Annabel looked over the girl's tank top and orange pants, so overwhelmed she had to clear her throat. "I remember, sweet Lucy." She hugged the girl tight. "And thank you."

"Nana helped me get dressed for tonight. I asked her if I should wear a pretty dress and she said, well, what do you want to wear, and I said I wanted to wear my Annabel outfit and showed her, and she said it would be just perfect."

Annabel smiled at Raina, then scooped up Lucy in her arms, balancing her on her hip. "Well, I guess we'd better sit down and let the cooking start."

Mayor Hickham poked his head out of the kitchen. "Okay. Essie and Clyde. The cook-off will commence in one minute. Please enter the kitchen." The mayor had used his beloved bullhorn to announce the rules ten minutes earlier on the porch. The ground beef had been delivered wrapped in one package that the mayor would split into two. Essie and Clyde would inspect the beef and make sure it was to their satisfaction. Then the mayor would announce that it was time to begin.

All in all, in about thirty minutes, a barbecued burger would end up changing Annabel's life.

Gram and her adversary shook hands at the kitchen door, then headed in. From their table, Annabel could hear the mayor say, "Three, two, one, start cooking!"

Annabel glanced at West, sitting on the far side of the table. He seemed preoccupied as he stared out the window, Lucy playing a card game with her grandparents. *I'm going to miss you both so much*, she thought.

The time passed so slowly. They'd only need around twenty minutes total to cook the burgers and make their sauce. Twenty minutes that moved like molasses.

Finally Mayor Hickham came out of the kitchen, Gram and Clyde behind him. The mayor held two plates, one in each hand. Under each plate was a name tag noting whose burger was whose, but Annabel would recognize Gram's brioche bun anywhere. The mayor set down the burgers at a stand in front of the dining room. Gram moved to the left, on her plate's side of the table, Clyde to the right.

The windows were all wide-open, people on the porch and in the backyard pressed close to hear.

"Okay, folks," the mayor began. "It's time for me to judge. You know I love Essie Hurley like a sister and you know I love Clyde Heff like a brother, but I love burgers even more than both of them, so you know I'll be honest." That got a big laugh from the crowd. "The best burger will win!" He took a bite of Clyde's burger, the expression on his face clear that it was good, as expected. Then he took a bite of Gram's and his face scrunched and he not too delicately spit out his bite into a napkin.

The crowd gasped.

What the heck—

"I'm sorry, Essie," the mayor said, quickly downing a gulp of water, "but someone must have sabotaged your burger because I'd say it's more salt than burger. There must be a tablespoon of salt in that one bite."

What? How could that be possible when both parties had inspected the beef?

The mayor took another sip of water, still grimacing from the bite of Essie's burger. "Either way, because of the rules, I'm very sorry to say that Hurley's Home-style Kitchen is hereby disqualified and the winner is Clyde Heff!"

Francie Heff started jumping up and down and squealing and the huge Heff family started blowing party horns as if it were New Year's.

Annabel glared at Francie jumping in her kitten heels. Francie must have poured a heap of salt on the meat. But how? It was impossible for Clyde's beef to be fine and Gram's to be full of salt. And anyway, Francie couldn't have sabotaged the burger; she hadn't been in the kitchen. The only people in the kitchen the entire time was Clyde Heff way on his side, Mayor Hickham in the center, keeping guard and watch, and Gram—

Gram?

Annabel whirled around, watching her grandmother shaking hands with Clyde Heff.

"I don't know what happened with your burger, Essie," Clyde said, "but rest assured it wasn't me or my daughter who had anything to do with it. I promise you that."

"I know that," Essie said. "I guess it's just one of those mysteries."

Not much of a mystery except for the *why*, Annabel thought.

As Stanton Heff made a big show of handing Clyde a check for the ten thousand dollars, mock-wiping his brow, Annabel stared at her grandmother, waiting for a moment to get her attention.

Finally Annabel took her grandmother's hand and led her over into the office and closed the door. "Gram. You sabotaged your own burger. Why? You gave up ten thousand dollars!"

"Okay, I did sabotage my burger with quite a bit of salt. I did it because you made a deal with West. That you'd stay for a few more months if we lost."

Annabel was even more confused. "Okay...?"

Essie took Annabel's hands. "And I know how much you love that man and his daughter. And I know that West loves you. I saw it in his face that day I told him he had my blessing. He only had my blessing because I know he loves you and always has. And I saw that love on his face today when he wished me luck. He'd rather do right by you and let you go than keep you at the ranch where he thinks you don't want to be, Annabel. He has no idea how much you love him."

"Maybe not," Annabel said. "I've tried not to show it."

"Oh, I'm sure West has tried not to show it too. But that man loves you like crazy."

Well, Annabel didn't believe that.

"A deal is a deal," Gram said, holding both Annabel's hands. "So off you go, back home to the ranch. Shoo, girl."

Oh, Gram.

Annabel headed out of the office, straining to see West in the crowd, which had started dispersing since Clyde called for a two-for-one burger celebration at Heffs. Big migration across the street.

But there on the porch swing was West and Lucy, Raina and Landon chatting on the sidewalk.

"Sorry Miss Gram didn't win," Lucy said, hopping up to hug Annabel.

"Well, sometimes you win even when you lose," West said, and Lucy looked up at him, wrinkling her face in confusion.

"Sweetie, come get a smoothie with Nana and Pop-Pop," Raina said. "I'm getting chocolate-coconut tonight."

"Ooh, me too!" Lucy said, racing over and grabbing both their hands as they swung her up.

West patted the seat next to him, and Annabel sat down, watching the throngs of people crowding in front of Clyde's Burgertopia.

"Everyone's talking," West said, "and wondering who sabotaged your grandmother's burger. Francie Heff is insisting on a re-cook-off so that her father can win fair and square, not by default. I can see that—everyone knows someone sabotaged that burger—"

"My gram did."

He stared at her. "What? Why?"

"She has this funny notion in her head about our marriage not being such a sham. She knows we made a deal that if Hurley's lost today, I'd stay at the ranch a few more months so that I wouldn't feel like I had to give you your money back so fast."

"Well, that's what I meant when I said sometimes you win when you lose. Hurley's didn't get the ten grand. So I get to keep you a little while longer."

Confused, Annabel looked into his driftwood brown eyes. Her grandmother couldn't be right about West loving her, but when had Gram Hurley ever been wrong, now that she thought about it? "I don't understand why, though. You'll never have to worry about Raina. You're a good cook. Everything is fine now. I'm the one who needs you. Hurley's needs you. You don't need me."

"Hell I don't." He turned toward her, taking her hands in his, his gaze intense on her. "I married you to keep Lucy from being taken away from me, yes. But I've always loved you, Annabel. I loved you that night in the barn. And I loved you on our wedding night when I made love to you. And I've loved you every day since. I just couldn't face it because I was so damned scared of losing someone I loved again."

Happiness zinged through every inch of Annabel's body. Seven years ago, he'd given her up *because* he'd loved her. "Oh, West. I love you too. I loved you seven years ago and I've loved you every day of our supposedly sham marriage."

He smiled and kissed her, passionately, possessively. Then he leaned back, cupping her face in his hands. "It's been very real to me too."

She took his hand, his gold wedding band shining

in the moonlight. "What would you have done if my grandmother hadn't cost herself the win?"

"I would have had the worst night's sleep, then marched into Hurley's in the morning and announced in the middle of the kitchen that I love my wife and want her to come home."

Annabel smiled. "Really?" Though, of course, she could see him doing just that.

"Heck yeah."

"So I guess this means I'm staying at the ranch for good," she said, sliding her arms around his neck.

"Well, now that I can make a decent meal and comb out my daughter's hair and Raina Dunkin is in my corner, I can take over a lot of what you were doing for Lucy. So if you want to cook for Hurley's or manage the restaurant or both, I'll be supportive of whatever you want to do, Annabel Hurley Montgomery."

She reached up her hand to touch his cheek, overwhelmed by how much she loved him. "You're a very good man, West Montgomery. And a very good husband."

He kissed her again and then they headed back inside Hurley's to thank one very wise grandmother.

Epilogue

A week later, at the re-cook-off on Saturday afternoon, it was standing room only again in Hurley's Homestyle Kitchen as everyone waited for the mayor, Gram, and Clyde to come out of the kitchen with the two barbecue burgers. The delicious aromas coming from the kitchen were almost unbearable, and since the restaurant would be closed for lunch for the cook-off, Annabel and Hattie had made a heap of appetizers and biscuits to keep folks satisfied.

A ping on Annabel's phone let her know she had a text. Detective Slater. *I'm on the porch. Can you come out?*

Annabel bit her lip and got up from her table, whispering to West that she'd be back in a minute. She weaved her way through the crowd to reach the cop. *Please have good news*, she thought.

Detective Slater nodded at her. "Annabel, I did see

your sister Georgia this past weekend in Houston. She seems just fine."

So why was his expression so strained, his voice tight?

"She seemed happy?" she asked, trying to read the handsome cop's face.

He looked away for a moment, his dark eyes distant. "Yeah. She did."

She waited for him to say something else, elaborate, but he didn't. "Okay, then. I'm very relieved to hear that. And thanks for checking on her. I feel a lot better."

After a quick "you're welcome" he headed down the porch steps. Annabel knew there was more to the story than the detective was letting on. But Georgia was okay. Happy even. And she'd come home when she could.

Annabel rejoined her table just as Mayor Hickham came out of the kitchen carrying two plates, each holding a scrumptious-looking burger, Gram and Clyde Heff behind him. As the mayor set the plates down on the podium, Gram moved to his left and Clyde to his right.

Mayor Hickham took a bite of Clyde's burger, his pleased sigh a clear sign that the burger was amazing, which made Annabel nervous. She and Clementine shared a worried glance, and West took hold of Annabel's hand and held it tightly.

Then the mayor bit into Gram's burger, that same sigh escaping, his eyes closing.

It seemed like slow motion as he took a sip of water, then bit into each burger again. Then again.

Finally he lifted his bullhorn. And declared the winner: a tie.

He said that both burgers were so darned good that he couldn't in good conscience possibly say one was better than the other. Clyde Heff wrote out a check to

Essie for the difference, five thousand dollars, and they shook on it. The crowd clapped and cheered, except for Francie Heff, who rolled her eyes and started talking her father's ear off about their next big publicity event. Everyone laughed when Clyde picked up a biscuit from his family's table, swiped some apple butter on it, handed it to Francie and told her "more eating, less talking." Even Francie smiled.

An hour later, the restaurant closed to the public till dinnertime, Annabel and Gram came out of the kitchen with a platter of winning barbecue burgers and a bunch of sides, from Lucy's favorite long, skinny fries to the spicy slaw West was always trying to make to perfection at home, to the corn bread Raina could never resist. They sat down at the big table by the window, the view of the Sweet Briar Mountains in the distance, West and Landon talking about the therapeutic riding program, Raina excitedly mentioning that she would be working with a young woman tomorrow afternoon at the ranch. Clementine made a smiley face out of ketchup for Lucy to dip her fries through, and Gram happily bit into her barbecue burger, cleared by her doctor to enjoy every last bite of it.

Annabel looked around the table, her heart soaring to be with her family—the Hurleys, the Montgomerys, the Dunkins—talking, laughing, eating, sharing. No matter where she was, with these people she'd be home.

* * * * *

MILLS & BOON®

Desire™

PASSIONATE AND DRAMATIC LOVE STORIES

A sneak peek at next month's titles...

In stores from 10th March 2016:

- **Take Me, Cowboy** – Maisey Yates *and*
  His Baby Agenda – Katherine Garbera

- **A Surprise for the Sheikh** – Sarah M. Anderson *and*
  Reunited with the Rebel Billionaire – Catherine Mann

- **A Bargain with the Boss** – Barbara Dunlop *and*
  Secret Child, Royal Scandal – Cat Schield

MILLS & BOON®

Helen Bianchin v Regency Collection!

40% off both collections!

Discover our Helen Bianchin v Regency Collection, a blend of sexy and regal romances. Don't miss this great offer - buy one collection to get a free book but buy both collections to receive 40% off! This fabulous 10 book collection features stories from some of our talented writers.

Visit **www.millsandboon.co.uk** to order yours!

0316_MB520

MILLS & BOON®

Why not subscribe?
Never miss a title and save money too!

Here's what's available to you if you join the exclusive **Mills & Boon® Book Club** today:

✦ *Titles up to a month ahead of the shops*
✦ *Amazing discounts*
✦ *Free P&P*
✦ *Earn Bonus Book points that can be redeemed against other titles and gifts*
✦ *Choose from monthly or pre-paid plans*

Still want more?
Well, if you join today, we'll even give you
50% OFF your first parcel!

So visit **www.millsandboon.co.uk/subs**
to be a part of this exclusive Book Club!

MILLS & BOON®

Why shop at millsandboon.co.uk?

Each year, thousands of romance readers find their perfect read at millsandboon.co.uk. That's because we're passionate about bringing you the very best romantic fiction. Here are some of the advantages of shopping at www.millsandboon.co.uk:

* **Get new books first**—you'll be able to buy your favourite books one month before they hit the shops

* **Get exclusive discounts**—you'll also be able to buy our specially created monthly collections, with up to 50% off the RRP

* **Find your favourite authors**—latest news, interviews and new releases for all your favourite authors and series on our website, plus ideas for what to try next

* **Join in**—once you've bought your favourite books, don't forget to register with us to rate, review and join in the discussions

Visit **www.millsandboon.co.uk**
for all this and more today!